Bad Endings

Bad Endings

stories by
Carleigh Baker

ANVIL PRESS · VANCOUVER · 2017

Anvil Press Publishers Inc.
P.O. Box 3008, Main Post Office
Vancouver, B.C. V6B 3X5 Canada
www.anvilpress.com

Library and Archives Canada Cataloguing in Publication

Baker, Carleigh, author
      Bad endings / by Carleigh Baker.

ISBN 978-1-77214-076-7 (softcover)

      I. Title.

PS8603.A449B33 2017   C813'.6   C2017-901136-7

Printed and bound in Canada
Cover design by Rayola.com
Cover illustrations by Katie Green
Author photo: Callan Field
Interior by HeimatHouse
Represented in Canada by Publishers Group Canada
Distributed by Raincoast Books

The Lee Maracle quote is from a tweet by Dallas Hunt.

The publisher gratefully acknowledges the financial assistance of
the Canada Council for the Arts, the Canada Book Fund, and the
Province of British Columbia through the B.C. Arts Council and
the Book Publishing Tax Credit

For my parents, who are only satisfied when
I'm being true to myself,
and for my brave sister.

"Fish is the hub of all our memories."

-LEE MARACLE

Contents

War of Attrition

My marriage is ending and it's my fault. In the other room, Andrew is snoring. I'm on the couch. Here is the buttery weight of polar fleece on bare skin, the entire length of my body unblemished by a goose bump. Try not to anticipate the cold. Squint at the dark window, listen for the rain, but only to harden against the inevitable. At five I get up: sweater, housecoat, slippers on the floor within reach. Pull them under the covers first. To turn on the gas fireplace is to risk making inside too comfortable. Kettle on while I dress for work: long underwear, fleece vest, wool sweater. Two layers of socks, even though that's not a good idea. Cuts off circulation, Andrew says.

Shell pants. Rubber boots. An old snowboarding jacket that was never used for snowboarding, Scotchgarded. A toque, and over that, a sou'wester, from when Andrew and I used to go sailing. Gloves with the fingers cut out. My last layer, the standard issue *Metropolitan News* vest with a pocket in the front for extra gloves and tissues, and a plastic panel in the back for today's paper.

Stand at the window with a cup of tea I'll only get a few sips into, and listen to Andrew. In the summer months, this time of day is clandestine and peaceful, but in the winter, it's just lonely. It is raining—misting really—a wet that will sneak up on me as the morning progresses. Moisture will collect on the SkyTrain supports over my head and drop down when the trains pass. Hit me in the face when I look up.

Down four flights of stairs in my rubber boots. Our suite is top floor, looks over the neighbourhood with a peekaboo view of the river during the day. I'll never be able to afford something like this after I leave him.

There are seldom any SkyTrain cops on the first train of the day. They've never hassled me on the way home either; the *Metropolitan* vest seems to have some kind of cloaking effect. With it on, I'm at the bottom of the food chain where I belong. Lana taught me to always keep an expired ticket, just in case. She says they're paying more attention to how guilty you look than the actual date on the ticket.

Lana is technically my rival; she hands out the *48 Hours* paper. She's good at working the system, which is very Russian of her, or at least that's what she says. I haven't met many Russians.

"Life is shit," she says in a Doctor Zhivago accent. We're pulling papers out of the morning stacks and folding them in half. "You marry doctor, move to Canada, then husband leave to have sex with nurses and you must marry butcher so you can stay. And for what? Canada. Is not so great here."

Her conviction compels me to nod. She claims to be past her prime but she has full lips and high cheekbones, and may have a supermodel body under her parka and shell pants. It's hard to tell. Wool hat with a pompom, pulled down low.

"It's ridiculous, this," she says, pointing at the pompom. "That's why I buy, to wear for this job. This ridiculous job." She considers. "And because was on sale."

We're both ready for the first rush. It's more efficient to prepare a bunch of papers in your vest and pull from there; running out in the middle of a rush could mean twenty or thirty losses. We both get a stack of about seven hundred every morning, left in a zap-strapped pile by the station entrance. I'm lucky to give out three hundred. Lana does at least twice that.

An older man with a pompadour approaches us from the station. "Svetlana!" he calls, and she offers him her cheek along with a paper. I hold out a *Metropolitan* and he ignores it.

"Is Tom," she says, waving as he retreats. "Very loyal to *48 Hours*." She can't resist a little sneer. We are rivals, after all.

"Ni how!" she calls to the Chinese men, the same Chinese men we see every day, and they say "Ni how miss," and bow a little when they take a paper from her. "Ni How! Have a nice day, have a nice day," she says. And as they walk off, "Chinese man have money, but very small penis."

"Don't you think that's just a stereotype?" I ask.

She shakes her pompom head. "Stereotype is truth."

I'm not leaving Andrew because I've met someone else. He didn't beat me up or call me names or cheat. I'm leaving because I don't want to work it out. We did try, once or twice. There's nothing to tell a divorce lawyer or my parents or friends, except maybe that he gave me too much. That's what he says, and I agree. I didn't have to work or cook or clean or worry about anything. Andrew took care of it all.

We both know that I can't leave until I have some kind of steady income. The *Metropolitan* was the only place willing to hire me right away, and not ask about the blank spot on my résumé covering the last five years. They put me at the 22nd Street station, not too far from where Andrew and I live. Every morning, there's a man who sings opera in Italian as he walks down the path toward me. He never takes a paper, but he bows and tips a non-existent hat. And a group of Korean girls in scrubs who all make eye contact with me and giggle, almost flirtatiously.

The Metro girl! the millworkers call out, on their way to Annacis Island. They still smell of sawdust, even in freshly washed clothes. If I tell them I'm having a slow day, they take two papers. On Valentine's day, one of the men gave me a carnation. I wore it in the zipper of my snowboarding jacket for a couple of hours, but I threw it away so Andrew wouldn't ask questions. Sometimes he picks me up in the car after my shift, even now that he knows it's over. This always gets a reaction from Lana.

"You crazy woman. You have good man, with car." She waves a *48 Hours* over her head. "And you leave. At least take car."

"I'm a terrible driver," I say.

"You crazy woman. You must take half."

"I don't want half." Lana would choke if she saw the stemless Riedel wine glasses and Denby cookware I'm walking away from. All these things that had seemed *absolutely necessary* at the time.

"Corrrrina—listen." She leans close, but continues to hand out papers with her right hand. "I tell you something." She takes a deep breath. "I—not actually Russian."

"Oh?"

"No, I lie to husband. He want Russian wife." She puts a hand on my arm and squeezes.

"Oh." We seem to be having a moment, but I'm not sure why.

"I am...Ukrainian." The word slips from her lips like a sigh. She pulls away as if I might smack her.

"He wouldn't have wanted a Ukrainian wife?"

"No." Lana sniffs. A big crowd just got off the train from King Edward, people are streaming past us. We work blindly with both hands, dispensing the morning news like vending machines. Lana's regulars are disappointed to not be receiving her full attention but she ignores this. "Nobody want Ukrainian wife! Ukrainian woman are good for prostitute only."

"Lana, that's impossible."

"Is true." Her jaw is set, cheeks sucked in. She pulls a tissue from her *48 Hours* vest and wipes her nose. "But Russians are the enemy of Ukrainia."

"Like the Canada and the US?"

She straightens. "You stupid in Canada, you ignorant," she says. "No offense."

"None taken."

"I give everything to get doctor husband." Her face darkens. "I give my true self. And then he sleep with nurses."

"I think I know what you're saying Lana," I say, and this at least is true. But it's not news to me. Only a crazy person would walk away from a man who treats her like a princess.

"Ahh Corrrina," she says, shoulders slumped. "If you really understand, you will not leave good husband."

At nine thirty, the rain turns to snow. Andrew's car pulls up, two lattes in the cup holders and the heat turned on high. I know he's angry, he hasn't stopped being angry, but he still does things like this. It feels too comfortable to settle in next to him, skin thawing with that prickly feel.

"How was it?" He smiles, but doesn't take his eyes off the road.

"The usual," I say. "Thanks for picking me up."

"You shouldn't walk home in the cold." He points to a bag in the back seat. "I'm going to stay at Tom's tonight." He pulls up to the house. "Don't you want the latte?" he says.

"I'm giving up coffee," I say. "And milk."

He has started to move some of my things under the stairs. There are spaces on the shelves where my Chairman Mao teapot and the photo of me trout fishing with my dad used to be. The photo will come with me in my backpack. The Chairman Mao teapot, wall clock, and propaganda poster will sit under the stairs until Andrew gives them away. I don't remember why I ever collected Mao stuff. I pick up a sweater of Andrew's from a chair and sniff, trying to kindle some emotion, but it's no good. My eyes well up, but the feeling passes before gravity can do its work. If anything, I'm just feeling sorry for myself. An email from Andrew contains a few links to cheap apartments on Craigslist. I should be the one to find a new place, since I'm walking away. He's even offered to pay for the first month.

I Google 'Russian-Ukrainian conflict.' My search produces radically different accounts, from Russia as the great patron of the Ukraine to its most bitter enemy, depending on who is telling the story. A page on the Holodomor—the Ukrainian famine in the 1930s—claims the Russian government starved the Ukrainian people in order to crush their independence movement. Millions of people died, but they didn't give in. Lana is right, I am ignorant. And spoiled. And probably crazy.

Absolute silence this morning. No rain. No snoring. I can't bring myself to sleep in the bed when he's not here, even though my feet hang off the end of the couch. The silence is so thick, my ears feel pressurized. I take vigorous deep breaths. In. Out. Inoutinoutinout. No time for breakfast, a handful of peanuts will do.

Andrew texts me while I'm on the train. *Found u a place. Think u should move out next wk.*

OK, I text back.

I'll help u move.

That's OK. He doesn't know I'm only taking a backpack. Keep it light enough to travel.

Lana always beats me to work; she only has to take the train one stop from Edmonds. There she is at the mouth of the station, lips curled into a pout. She's holding a bunch of helium balloons.

"For you," she says, and presents them with a bow, and for an awful moment I think they're from Andrew, or maybe the guy with the carnation—but no. "*Metro* manager came by, left for you."

"What the hell am I supposed to do with them?"

Lana snorts. "Hold them while you give paper, and say *M for Metropolitan, your letter of quality.*"

"What? What does that even mean—"

"—No, excuse me, you must yell," she says. "You must yell *M for Metropolitan, your letter of quality!*"

"What?"

"Yell it."

"Lana, is this even real?"

"Yell it, Corrrrina," she commands, tying a couple of balloons to the hood of my jacket. "You want leave comfortable life, work here with losers—"

"—You're a pretty hot loser."

"I know." She doesn't blink. "Could have been hot loser prostitute, instead marry loser doctor."

"I read about the Ukraine last night," I say. "Holodomor."

"Russia take everything, but they can't break spirit!" She thrusts an arm in the air. "But don't change subject."

"M for *Metropolitan*." I take a balloon and tie it to her pompom. Another around her elbow.

"Well? I don't hear you yell." Lana ties balloons to both my braids and the string on the sou'wester.

"CAN I GET A *48 HOURS* HERE?" somebody calls.

Lana points to a stack on the sidewalk "It not six o'clock yet, get it yourself!" And then to me—"Well?"

I cringe. "M for *Metropolitan*, your letter of quality."

"Terrible." She snorts. "You want lose job? Go back to nice husband with car?"

"You can have him," I say.

"What?"

"You can have my husband. And his car."

"And?" Lana tugs on my braid balloons and I want to smack her.

"And M for *Metropolitan*, your letter of quality!" A group of power-suited commuters look at me and snicker. My throat hurts.

"Better," she says. "How you feel?"

"Like an idiot."

"Then this is life you choose."

Around 8:00 a.m., the temperature drops a little more. I start to shiver. Sometimes this serves my purpose, since people feel bad and take a paper. It's a fine line, tip the scales too far towards guilt and they'll get annoyed and avoid me. If I can keep smiling like a trooper, I'll probably do pretty well in the last hour. But the temperature keeps dropping until my head starts to feel light and the balloons start to droop. People trudge right past me with their coat collars turned up. A man swoops past Lana and me with his teeth bared, holding tight to his pregnant wife like he's her body-guard.

"It's the newspaper beggars," he says. Neither of them make eye contact with us.

Lana stands still for a minute. "You want some ginger tea?" she asks me.

"I'm okay."

"Me too," she says.

I see Andrew's car pull up again, just before nine thirty.

"Lana," I say, "I'm going to take off a few minutes early." I slip away from Andrew, into the station, taking the stairs two by two.

"But, good husband!" Lana calls after me. "You crazy! You cray-zeee!"

The people on the train are staring. My phone is buzzing in my front pocket, and limp balloons hang from my braids. The heat is cranked and my feet are sweaty from two pairs of socks. The train pulls into Columbia, the stop closest to home. The doors open and close, but I'm still riding.

The Modern Intimate

'm grating carrots, organic I think, and the stove is pre-heating. I've got a vegan baked-oatmeal recipe though neither of us are vegan. It just seems a lot healthier. Eric's been wanting to ditch the pancakes, and I can get behind that. I suppose if I was really on-board the health train I'd be making us poached eggs and steamed greens, but god, I'm not perfect. I already ran ten kilometres this morning, and it's not even 6:00 a.m. There has to be some reward.

The carrots are thin and kind of rubbery (definitely organic) so I have to push hard against the grater, and I keep shearing off my nails. Damn. Eric loves my hands. I like them too, though I didn't put much effort into my nails until I met him. They just grow, and I let it happen. Now there are mani/pedi afternoons, and a spare couple of bottles of polish at home for emergency touch-ups. Right now, they're Maximum Midnight. Totally badass. I pull the grater up slowly and pick out the black nail pieces. Gross. After a thorough inspection, I mix the certified nail-free carrots in with rolled oats, vanilla, and some almond milk, which I was happy to switch to for Eric, even though milk doesn't bother me.

Agave syrup for sweetener; is it really healthier? Who knows. It feels healthier. I add half of what the recipe suggests, then a little more. Then a little more. Three times the recommended amount of cinnamon and nutmeg, and a ton of fresh ginger. Pat it out in the pan, sprinkle nuts on top. Bam! In the oven for thirty minutes. Add a little vanilla to some coconut cream, put it in the fridge to chill. Vegan whipped cream. Better than the real deal? Maybe. It is pretty good.

Eric is upstairs in my room, still sleeping. His place is a true bachelor, a downtown ultra-compact, so we usually go out for meals when we stay there. But I share a big house with roomies, so getting up early to make breakfast doesn't disturb him. He's going to Ottawa for a conference, and breakfast is kind of my way of telling him I'll miss him. We've been dating for a while, six months, though we usually only see each other once a week. He's so busy. I find I miss him more and more when he goes away, even though I should probably be getting used to it as we become more comfortable with each other. Which I'm pretty sure is happening. This is the first time he's spent the night before flying out. Seems like we're getting closer. As much as I feel like a lame fifties housewife saying it, I want to be closer. I've been doing stupid things like doodling our names together when I should be working. Carrie and Eric. Carrie and Eric Johnson. Carrie and Eric Johnson-McGill. A truly modern woman would demand a hyphenated last name. This is the kind of stupid shit I did in my teens, then scoffed at in my twenties. Now here I am in my thirties, still not married, mooning over a dude again. God. This wasn't in the life plan.

I draw a sink full of warm water and add a squirt of the earth-happy, biodegradable soap my roomie always buys. It smells like lemongrass, and the warm water is a comfort in the chilly house. I should have put socks on. I've been working in dim light, but now I flip the wall switch with an elbow, just enough light to make sure the dishes are clean. I hate it when people come into a room I'm working in and turn the light on over my head smugly, like I'm too stupid to not have figured it out myself. I choose the darkness. I hang on to it for as long as possible.

Eric will be up soon. He sets his cellphone alarm right after we have sex at night and never hits snooze in the morning. He doesn't like lying around. He doesn't like morning sex. He goes from zero to sixty within minutes of opening his eyes.

* * *

Eric has perfected the art of texting while darting through a crowd. It's all in the peripheral vision, the ability to focus on two things at once. Necessity precipitated this skill, the need for efficiency, not the lame desire to be connected to Facebook buddies 24/7. The flight was delayed, so he needs to let his seven o'clock dinner downtown know that he'll be late. They've got a table for twenty reserved, and his tardiness will mean he gets a crappy seat on the perimeter, but nobody can hear each other at these things anyway. Pre-conference meet-ups are just a message to people that you're here; nobody walks around with their business cards out like a bunch of thirsty car salesmen. All you do at dinner is make plans for drinks, see who is going to be back at the convention centre bar; that's when you get a chance to talk. While you're having drinks you can excuse yourself twice without seeming weird, nip into the hallway where the bathrooms are and text ahead to see who's back at the hotel bar, which means getting another connection in before bed. That doesn't always work out; three connections in one day is kind of like the Holy Grail.

Expensive shoes *click click click* on the terminal floor. Eric has a new pair of Magnannis. There's a Starbucks kiosk right before the exit. Perfect. That's new since the last time he was here. The barista eyes his Italian suit and bats her lashes at him a little. She must see guys like him all day. Or maybe not quite like him: he's young to be this well dressed, young for the office he has at City Hall. He pats down his hair, notices a little spot on the back of his head where it's sticking out. He slept funny on the plane. He'll fix it in the cab. Takes his Americano from the grinning barista with an "aw shucks" shrug. He hates drinking coffee, but all good habits dissolve for the duration of a business trip. Again, necessity. He hates drinking alcohol too, empty calories. But it's what's done; you look like a prig if you don't have a drink in your hand. This conference will be all beer and sliders, not a vodka soda in sight, even though the same group of people might travel to Toronto and it's Nolet's and ceviche. Ottawa is mom-and-pop authenticity, bars with names like The Pig and Whistle. The Fox and Syringe. The bloat and heart attack.

Eric's phone buzzes. *Trichloroisocyanuric acid*, says the subject line of an email. There are twenty-five new messages and they're all from the city.

"Westin, Shaw Centre," Eric says to the cabbie, already absorbed in his phone. Something about a chemical fire in the port. Jesus. He's been out of town for five hours. It's twenty minutes to the hotel, enough time to proofread the media releases that have already been drafted. Tweet out emergency procedures and messages to people on the East-side to stay indoors. Three words, *I'M ON IT*, arrive in a text from the director of communications, who undoubtedly knows that Eric has landed by now. At the bottom of the list there's an email from Carrie, *Bedtime Story* in the subject line. She's attached a video. He gets a little bit hard at the thought of what it could be, but that makes him anxious so he stops thinking about it. Got to start things off here with the right kind of energy, the kind that looks effortless. Eric takes a couple of breaths and does one of the mindfulness exercises he was taught by the mayor himself. Closes his eyes and moves through the inside of his body from head to toes, just focussing on himself. Awareness is a blessing and a curse. There's the potential for more self-control, but sometimes Eric just becomes exponentially more aware of how uncomfortable he is. The Magnannis pinch his feet. His new Omega has got a hold of some arm hair. He misses Carrie, maybe, a little.

"Westin," the cabbie says. Eric looks up, surprised. Hands the man his corporate card.

The restaurant can't decide whether it's an Italian bistro or an English pub, but the familiar smell is somewhat comforting. Fried stuff, oregano, beer. Eric looks past the buxom host and sees a slim, tanned arm shoot up from one of the tables and wave. Phone buzzes in his back pocket as he navigates the sea of business suits. He moves it to his jacket pocket and glances at the message but he can't make it out. Best not to be caught with your phone out too much while you're mingling. Other people do it, but Eric thinks it looks tacky.

The arm belongs to Mathilde, a city planner from Montreal.

"Be thankful I saved you a seat," she says. "Look at the duds on the perimeter."

"Thanks," Eric says, kissing Mathilde on the cheek. He doesn't recognize the guys at the end of the table, but they do look like duds. Beer guts and combovers. He's happy to start the evening with Mathilde. She's got about a decade on Eric but you'd never guess it; she must bathe in virgin's blood. They bonded years ago at an event in Toronto, she was surreptitiously watering down a drink with San Pellegrino, and Eric thought this seemed like a good idea as well. Switching from a strict diet to conference party mode requires strategy.

There's little time at these events to chat someone up just because they're beautiful, but Mathilde had connections to a big consulting firm Eric had been eyeing, and she'd been interested in Eric's work on urban bike lanes. They'd talked late into the night about green initiatives and the looming transit strike in Vancouver. After that, when the watered down drinks finally took hold, they talked about other things.

"It's hard to get close to anyone when you do this work," she'd said, in a creamy accent. "Impossible, really." She pointed her head down and lifted her eyes at him.

Eric had felt like maybe he could have made a move then. But for some reason he didn't.

The shipping container that is currently on fire and blanketing East Vancouver in fumes comes from China, and was on its way inland. Last year, over five hundred containers of trichloroisocyanuric acid passed through the port without catching fire. *Set the number of accident-free days back to zero*, somebody in communications quips in an email. Calls are pouring into the city from people with respiratory problems, claiming to be at death's door.

Tell them to call a doctor, Eric texts to the communications assistant. *Honestly, people just lose their minds*. He googles *Trichloroisocyanuric acid health risks* and scans quickly. An industrial cleaning agent. Harmful when inhaled. Explosion hazard. Maybe he should catch a flight home, he thinks, as he walks back to Mathilde.

"Who's on your hotlist tonight?" she asks, scanning the table. City councilors, angel investors, urban-development consultants, and a charismatic guy Eric recognizes as a speaker from a TED conference last year, but can't remember what the talk was about.

"Unless something's changed, I'm meeting Trevor and Marlis from Dingo after this," Eric says. His phone is buzzing again. Dingo is a new consultancy firm from Los Angeles that specializes in green space. "They've made overtures to the city recently about the CP Rail corridor along Arbutus."

"I know all about that. Community gardens ripped out," Mathilde says. "The locals don't like it."

"The locals don't like any change, ever," Eric says. "But it continues."

"Story of my life," Mathilde says. Eric isn't sure exactly what she's referring to, but it's a tidy exit. Short, clean conversations are best. Eric orders some kind of microbrew pale ale from the impossibly gorgeous waitress. Fettucini Alfredo, but a pass on the garlic toast. Check the phone one last time, under the table, like that fools anyone. *Fire's out. No fatalities.*

Okay. Time for small talk and backslapping.

By the end of the evening, Eric's figured out that the TED guy wrote a book called *Strong Cities*, which Eric read and loved. They make a tentative plan for beers after the second panel discussion tomorrow, to be firmed up later via text. The guy tells Eric to bring his friend, and nods at Mathilde. Eric grins in spite of himself. Mathilde would eat him for breakfast. He tells the *Strong Cities* guy he'll do his best. Marlis and Trevor from Dingo cancel, which is annoying, but Eric is exhausted anyways, and bloated from the beer.

"Goodnight, gorgeous," he says to Mathilde, in the hallway by the bathrooms, kissing her on both cheeks this time. There's an ornately framed print of *Dogs Playing Poker* behind her.

She smacks his ass, barely looks up from her phone. "Good luck with the corridor. And the fire. God, just read about it."

"It's out," Eric says. "No fatalities."

Back at the hotel, he scans the bar to see if there are any familiar faces, but it's pretty dead. A bit of a relief, really. He'll have a bath, which he never does at home, and catch up on the news. His room is away from the street, as he requested, though they didn't have his usual suite. Too bad. Familiarity keeps the nerves in check.

The neutrality of a hotel room is one of Eric's favourite things. The shower is compact but the tub is oversized. He brushes his teeth, and starts the water running. There's a couple of little bottles of bubble bath, so he pours them in under the tap and foam fills up the tub. The water turns the colour of a tropical lagoon. Chemicals. But the effect is somewhat pleasing. He flips down the lid on the toilet and sets his laptop on it, picks out a playlist. Mostly classical tonight. Takes off his suit and hangs it carefully, folds socks and underwear and puts them in the bag he keeps in his suitcase for dirty clothes. That's when he finds the Tupperware container with a heart drawn on the lid.

Two big slices of baked oatmeal. Carrie will be asleep by now; she almost always gets up early to run. He admires that about her. He takes a bite of the oatmeal even though it means he has to brush his teeth again. She is sweet. Carrie is so sweet. He's just not feeling it. Or really, he thinks he should be feeling it more. He remembers the email she sent and goes back to the bathroom, turns the water off. Opens the movie she sent him on his laptop and her sweet face appears. He wonders again if she's going to get naked, but she says she's going to read him a bedtime story, which of course is what the subject line had promised. It's some kids story about a bunny who is threatening to run away. His helicopter mom threatens to follow him around wherever he goes. With her dark eyes darting from the book to the screen, Carrie reads something about turning into a boat, and sailing the sea looking for him. The bunny, that is. Not Eric.

He lets himself down slowly into the bath. Phone in hand. He should check email, see how the damage control is going back home. But he clicks on the little orange flame icon instead. He's been chatting with a girl on Tinder for a few weeks now. She's beautiful, half Vietnamese. Annalee. It's probably time to act, Eric thinks. He'll ask her out when he gets home. It will help him power through the end of things with Carrie. He swipes through a few profiles first, looking for anything new and exciting. Photos of smiling faces: swipe right if you like what you see, left if you don't. If both parties swipe right, then you have a match. Women are experts at looking beautiful in their profile photos, so it all gets a little boring after a while. They all do yoga. They all love travel. Eric can't remember the last time he travelled for pleasure. He and Carrie had talked about going to Iceland. On the laptop, Carrie finishes her bedtime story. "Sweet dreams," she says. Saccharine.

Eric has a shortlist of Tinder matches, no sense messing around with a cast of thousands. He scrolls up and down, but Annalee's not there. He checks again, closes Tinder and opens it. Gone. That means she removed him as a match. After two weeks of chatting! She hadn't used her real name. They hadn't even exchanged numbers. So basically, she's gone forever.

Eric leans back in the tub. This is unexpected. He'd liked texting with her.

"Shit." He focuses on tangible things: warmth, his wrinkled toes, blistered from the Magnannis. Bubbles. The syrupy smell of blue lagoon bubble bath. A new text from Carrie: *did u get my email?*

* * *

I can't sleep and I feel stupid; I thought for sure Eric would call before bed. The bedtime story I emailed was silly, but surely he'd be touched by the effort. It's an adorable story— *The Runaway Bunny*—about a petulant little bunny who's testing his mom's devotion, but she keeps reassuring him that she'll always be there for him. God, maybe that was way too cheesy, or it sent some kind of weird matriarchal vibe to him. Carrie, you dumbass. He's asleep by now— guaranteed. He hates getting less than seven hours of sleep. I guess I just *assumed* he'd call, then *expected* a call, and now here I am. Am I angry? Don't think so. There's this sensation of having all the blood sucked out of my extremities, my head and hands tingle, and there's an uncomfortable pressure in my core. Nervous. That's what I am. All these little signs from the last few weeks keep popping up—I didn't see them as signs at the time, but now they seem relevant, unavoidable. The night he cancelled plans to go to the Cinematheque at the last minute; I was already downtown. That time we bumped into each other on Main Street and he seemed like he couldn't wait to get rid of me. The fact that we've been dating for *six months* and he still can't make more time to see me every week. How did I not put the pieces together? I feel stupid because I am stupid. Shit.

There's a pack of Camel menthols in a basket beside the bed, and I'd promised myself I'd throw them away, but I didn't. I'll feel like crap on my run tomorrow. Whatever. Throw on a sweater and socks and pad downstairs. Light the cig on the stove element and run out the door quickly. The first drag is so good. I realize how scrunched up my shoulders are. Another drag and I'm a little light-headed, probably better to sit down.

It's dark. There's a laurel bush around the whole house; it's over ten feet high and several feet thick. Impenetrable. It's quiet, like, 5:00 a.m. quiet, like the beautiful still moments before my morning run. I want to cry, but that seems stupid, preemptive. No dumping has actually occurred yet. But in one definitive *whoosh* the certainty that it will happen has engulfed me, even through the comfortable haze of the nicotine.

Phone's in my pocket. Damn. I don't want to do this. I don't want to do it but I know I'll feel better. I just want to feel better so I can go to sleep.

I was going to throw the cigs away, around our fourth

month dating, when I assumed we were getting serious, and I was going to uninstall Tinder. I did neither. Now I know why. It's not like I have to message anyone, just swipe at a few faces. See who swipes me back. Nothing soothes the burn of a preemptive dump like a smoke, and a preemptive search for somebody new.

Buddy Frank's Steps to Success

The ice cream bucket ashtray is overflowing. Half-smoked Matinée extra-milds from Ella's attempt to cut back. Fully-smoked Craven Ms—a more recent attempt to nauseate herself into quitting via menthol. Both plans failed, and the whole thing's been abandoned until after Christmas. There's a quit smoking book Ella saw on TV that looked good, *Buddy Frank's Three Steps to Success* or something like that. But it's expensive, and who knows if these things are going to work?

Vi's butts outnumber Ella's two to one; she never talks about quitting. Most days Ella and Vi sit out in the carport, on a couple of plastic lawn chairs, bundled up against the cold. Puffing away. Vi nattering on. Nearly all the Gemstone outpatients smoke, or at least, everyone that Ella knows.

Ella empties the bucket into a garbage bag. An inch of brown ice at the bottom falls out in one piece, like aspic. Ew. Vi would triple-bag. *Those poor, dear dustmen,* she'd say, in her faux-British accent. But Vi's not here. She's at her family's place until after New Year's. She set up all the decorations and a hokey plastic tree before she left, wouldn't let Ella touch a thing. That was fine, but Ella's been thinking about the chocolates Vi left under the tree. Five different boxes, arranged alphabetically. She could eat them—just the Almond Roca—and tell Vi that Prince Edward came by and took them. Said thanks, but he just wanted the Almond Roca. She considers it—seriously considers it. Lights another cig.

A white car pulls into the duplex down the street. That'll be the outpatient worker, doing the holiday rounds, making sure nobody's suicidal. Must be handy that they can hit so many people in such a small radius—the neighbourhood is a Gemstone ghetto. Rent is cheap here on the Eastside, and disability payments are skimpy. Ella met a few neighbours when Ms. Zyprexa had a grease fire last month. Ms. Z was discharged from Gemstone around the same time as Ella. Zyprexa is a drug, of course. Ella forgets most people's names, but usually remembers what meds they're on. In the hospital, that gets discussed long before talk turns to the weather. It's comfortable common ground, like the hockey game last night or whatever.

After one last dramatic exhale—a whoosh of white into cold air—Ella butts out and goes inside to tidy up before the worker gets to her place. It's supposed to be helpful, but she feels like the workers are judging her when they come over, checking to see if she's keeping up with things even when Vi's away.

The ground floor is unfinished: a wood skeleton stuffed with pink insulation, cement floor, wires running every-where. Damn washing machine is banging away; Ella unwinds the towels from the agitator and starts it again. Hauls the vacuum upstairs.

When Vi is home she cleans constantly. It's like the germs know she's gone, Ella thinks, wrinkling her nose at a new mildew spot on the ceiling. She scrubs at it with a disposable cleaning wipe. Whatever the disinfectant is, it makes her hands burn. When Ella gets her own apartment she's going to spend the first month eating chips in her pyjamas, dropping crumbs on the floor and laughing.

Ella left Gemstone House nine months ago. Her discharge worker was a guy with darting eyes and a dozen different Winnie-The-Pooh ties. None of the other workers even wore collared shirts, let alone ties. Ella asked him if he dressed up to look more mature, since he was only twenty-six. Two years younger than her. She told him the ties weren't helping.

"My clients love them," he told her.

"They're humouring you," she said.

He laughed, long and loud enough to clarify that *he* was in fact humouring *her*. But he'd gone to bat for her, and convinced Mental Health to keep her in assisted living for a year. They had one spot left.

"There's nothing to worry about," the worker assured Ella. "But Vi is . . ." He rolled his pen between his hands and studied the ceiling. "She's been through three roommates in six months."

"Fourth one's the charm?" Ella said. She needed a cig. It didn't matter how high-maintenance Vi was. After three years of scheduled meals, meds, and therapy, Ella was totally not ready for the real world.

Vi always insists that the vacuuming be done in straight lines, alternating directions like a golf course. Ella follows the pattern now, even though she's bound to mess it up long before Vi sees it. She considers that, and pushes the vacuum diagonally across the room, but it makes her pulse race.

Back to lines. Sometimes she really understands where Vi is coming from. Order is calming, even when it's extreme.

It took three therapists to get Ella's diagnosis right. In fact, when she was admitted to Gemstone, Ella's diagnosis was the same as Vi's. Serious case, schizoaffective. Now she's, what? Not so serious. What looked like psychosis was actually anxiety. Anxiety is curable, or at least, manageable. With the right tools. Order is an anxious-person thing. Control is another anxious-person thing. But the two aren't always the same. Listening to idiots rant about how OCD they are because they straighten paintings on the wall makes Ella want to punch something. Who *doesn't* want straight paintings? When Ella was in the hospital, her sister Carol had gone to clean out Ella's old apartment, and found three hundred and seven stacked pizza boxes, in various states of decay. Two hundred and seven empty cans of Coke in the bathtub. "What are they for?" she'd asked, over the phone. "Crafts?"

Ella cringed, but the doctors had told her to be as honest as possible with her family about what a freak she was. "I thought something bad would happen if I threw them away."

"What, exactly?" Carol's voice suggested a smile, or maybe a rictus. Ella couldn't tell.

"I'm a little unclear on that part."

And that was true, Ella had always been confused by her actions. The collecting, the stacking, the counting and recounting. But it made her heart stop racing, which told her brain that she was making the right choices. On the winning team. Whatever.

Vi is different, and that's an understatement. She's got anxiety issues, but she also has a whole cast of characters inside her head. Sometimes it's old roommates, but mostly it's the Royals. She talks to the Royals a lot. The chocolates under the Christmas tree are for Prince Edward; he's Vi's "husband." Ella's not sure if he's supposed to be *the* Prince Edward, Earl of Wessex, with the weak chin and smarmy smile. For all of Vi's talk of him, she's never described his looks, and Ella's never asked. She's always imagined more of a Disney-like cartoon: a two-dimensional man with perfect hair and white gloves and a gentle smile. But who knows, maybe he looks like Buddy Frank, the quit smoking guru: bleached-white teeth, spray tan, permed hair dyed black. A picture of health.

Vi talks to the prince on a cellphone she never charges, in a bubbly baby voice quite different from the imperious tone she saves for Ella. She writes him letters and posts them on her door. One of the reasons Vi's always cleaning is because the Royals could drop by at any time. Best to be prepared.

* * *

Ella gets exactly two hours with her family on Boxing Day: Mom, Dad, and Carol. They've slotted her in between their own Christmas plans. She knows she should be grateful— they've driven almost two hours to see her, since she didn't want to take the bus home. The Greyhound at Christmas is as depressing as Gemstone was—more really, since the healthcare workers used to at least make an effort at merriness. Her parents visited once a week at Gemstone, and have continued to do so since she moved in with Vi, but this is the first time Carol has been to the house. Ella watches Carol appraise the place: Vi's dust-free collection of commemorative Lady Di plates, oceans of hand sanitizer, the hospital booties Vi insists guests wear even when they take their shoes off. The couch that's so hard you bounce back a little when you try to sit on it. That's what Carol does, bounces back, her lipstick mouth forming an O as her bum comes to rest.

"That's a lot of chocolate," she says, looking under the Christmas tree. Ella doesn't bother explaining. She knows Carol is sneaking peeks at her expanded waistline. There have been vast changes in Ella's body lately, thanks to changes in meds. Off the antipsychotics. Onto the antidepressants. Lower doses of some things, higher doses of others. She'll sleep a day away, then ride an insomniac wave for three days. Besides the walk to the 7-Eleven—two hundred and seventy steps each way, all with the head-sinking, stomach-rising sensation that accompanies leaving the house—exercise is unthinkable.

The family's brought gifts: soap and scented candles and strawberry-infused vinegar. The kind of presents you get at office parties, Ella thinks. She's bought them whatever she could afford on a disability cheque: dollar-store journals and pens, rainbow novelty socks. Everyone seems satisfied, they probably hadn't expected much. After gifts, Dad goes outside to shovel the driveway, and Mom does the dishes. Ella and Carol sit across from each other, sipping from the bottles of water Vi keeps stocked. Crinkling the plastic.

"I've given notice," Ella says.

"Moving out?" Carol raises an eyebrow. "Where?"

"Anywhere that takes fatty nutso chain-smokers," Ella says. "Lemme know if you hear of something."

Carol laughs. "You're not nutso." She laughs a little harder, even though it's not all that funny.

"Have you heard of Buddy Frank?" Ella asks Carol.

"He's amazing," Carol says. "It's how I quit. I'll lend you his book."

"Thanks," Ella says. She finds it hard to imagine Carol ever smoking now, but she remembers seeing her in the Gemstone parking lot, puffing away before coming upstairs to visit. She'd always smell like hand sanitizer and perfume and mint gum. And smoke. Ella opens her laptop and shows Carol some YouTube videos, a bunch of clips of cats falling off stuff. Carol loves cats. Anything to keep laughing.

Before they leave, Ella finds Carol bent over at Vi's door, reading her letters to the Royals. Layers of paper, crude scrawls on foolscap. It's the only part of the house Vi allows to remain a mess.

Dear Royals,
Please forgive Vi for hanging up on Queen Mum
after Prince Edward forgot to eat his apple.

It's been a while since Ella's looked at the letters, even though their bedrooms are right across the hall from each other. There must have been some significant apple drama, because another letter says *GET LOST, APPLES*. Ella remembers Vi bringing home a discount bag of bruised Spartan apples in September. She put a sign on them: *For Queen*. When they started to attract fruit flies, Ella threw the apples out. Vi didn't seem to notice.

"These people aren't real," Carol says.

"Duh."

Carol looks up. "Did you ever do that?"

"Write letters to the royal family? No, dumbass. We're not all the same—"

"—You knew who I was the whole time?"

"At Gemstone? Of course."

"You knew who I was, always."

"I still do," Ella says, "you're a dumbass."

"Listen, dumbass, if you quit smoking, you could come and live with me," Carol says.

Ella tries to look thankful. "I'll keep it in mind."

* * *

Ella has an apartment viewing in two hours. She blow-dries her hair and puts on her makeup, but it looks too heavy when she's finished, so she washes her face and starts again. She'll leave out the bronzer; who has a tan this time of year anyway? It looks a little better the second time. She wipes off the liner and draws it on again.

The last time Ella lived alone, things didn't go so well. The pizza boxes and the Coke cans. Some days she got out of bed, to get smokes. Or if the WiFi went down, and she had to reset the router in the living room. She told her parents to stop visiting, at least for a few weeks. That's what she said to them.

She'd tried to kill herself before, but not with the same resolve. Before it had been handfuls of pills. She got dressed and put on her coat and walked across the street to the river. People usually put rocks in their pockets, she thought. But the Thompson has a hell of a current. It would probably be enough.

There was an older woman on the beach, kind of rough looking, maybe homeless. "You don't want to do that," she said, when Ella waded in.

It was November, the water was brutally cold, but Ella had expected that.

"You don't want to do that," the woman repeated. "Hey."

"Yes, I do." Ella was surprised at the way the words choked her.

She took a couple more steps, her feet unsteady, the brown Thompson River swirling around her knees. Maybe she should just jump for it, she thought, wondering how long it would take to die if she didn't sink. Maybe she did need the rocks.

"No, hon, you really don't. I've been there," the woman said, and to Ella's surprise, she took off her jacket and waded in.

"Stop," Ella said, but it came out more like *slurp!* She was shivering now, up to her thighs, legs giving out. And when they did give out a few seconds later, that woman jumped after her and hung on.

It was awkward and jerky, Ella trying to protest and bat the woman away, the woman exhaling gin breath in Ella's face, and in the middle of everything, Ella deciding she didn't actually want to die.

"Swim to shore," the woman said, her wet hair wrapping across Ella's face and making it hard to breathe. "Swim to shore."

"Okay," Ella said. "Okay."

Of course there were other people there by then: some guy walking his dog, a couple of teenagers with wide eyes who offered Ella their jackets. The guy with the dog had called an ambulance. And eventually, after a few days in the psych ward, someone had called Gemstone. She never did see that drunk lady again, but Ella calls her Shirley.

* * *

Ella's going to have to get on that bus if she wants to see the apartment. Her jeans feel tight—too tight—but that might be because she's been living in sweats. Even her socks feel tight; can feet get fat? She decides on a skirt with an elastic waistband. Doesn't let herself look in the mirror again. She takes one more swipe at that mould on the ceiling with a Windex-soaked rag, and wipes up the hair on the bathroom floor. Cleans the toilet. That should make Vi happy.

When Vi got back after New Year's she packed up all the Christmas decorations, *tut-tutting* over the dust on the glass ornaments. She was disappointed that Prince Edward hadn't been by. It sounds like they're having it out right now—Ella can hear Vi sobbing in her room. She's glad she didn't eat the Almond Roca.

"Be back soon, Vi." Ella knocks lightly on the door.

"Cheerio," Vi calls out shakily, a disembodied voice.

Ella wonders if, after she's moved out, Vi will hallucinate arguments with her about whether it's okay to run the washing machine at 5:00 a.m., or use hand sanitizer on the dishes. She hopes not. The Royals are demanding enough.

Shoes on. When Ella leaves the carport, the head-sinking, stomach-rising sensation will start. Deep breaths will help, though at first they'll make her heart race. This happens all the time, even when she's just going for cigs. *I am not going to pass out. I am not going to throw up.* Mantras her therapist says might work someday if she keeps using them. Ella doesn't want to smoke, since every single apartment on Craigslist specified *non-smokers only*. She's got to get that book from Carol.

Thirteen steps out of the carport, and her stomach clenches. There's a half-smoked butt on Vi's lawn chair; Ella takes a couple quick drags and throws some gum in her mouth. Better. Snow crunches under her feet. She thinks about going back for her boots, or just going back, period. But Ella sees the Tranquille Road bus coming, and it's only thirty-five more steps to the bus stop. When she gets back, she'll make a stupidly big bowl of popcorn and watch a movie with Vi.

Shoe Shopping with the Cash Poor

Divorce is something you should look good for, like wearing a suit when you fly in case you get upgraded to business class. The last time Travis and I saw each other was at the courthouse. I was dressed to impress: skirt, heels, and a Hawaiian Tropic tan. I was hoping he'd wear a suit, but he hadn't even bothered with a collared shirt.

Travis knew I'd been to Maui, which was creepy because he'd blocked me on Facebook. Lord knows his friends and family weren't speaking to me. I'd had an affair. The excommunication process was swift and thorough. I asked if he had any vacation plans. He told me exactly how long it was going to take him to pay off our debts. Two years, nine months, and eighteen days: longer than the actual marriage. I told him I didn't pay for my trip, which was true. He understood what this meant, and his face crumpled in for a moment as he pictured me rolling around on a beach with some guy—his replacement. I bit my lip. Then we went in to sign the papers.

He was in a better mood once it was over. So simple with no kids, nothing to contest. He was keeping the apartment we rented in Coal Harbour, and the BMW we leased. So, just a bunch of signatures and a three-month wait.

"Let's get some tea," he said. "I found this place."

I thought he meant a cup of tea, and that sounded like a nice parting gesture, so I let him drag me all the way down Georgia Street on my ridiculous heels. He made a big show of not opening the door for me and I tried not to roll my eyes.

The store looked like a *frou-frou* apothecary. Brown glass jars and tin boxes lined up on floor-to-ceiling shelves. Single-serve bags of dried herbs wrapped up to look like French macaroons and arranged in pastel patterns. Samples in glass teapots spiced up the place with smells of ginger and cardamom.

Two impeccably groomed guys in suits behind the counter. *Tea Sommelier*, their name tags said. If everything else hadn't been a sign I should have run out of there, that was it.

"You go ahead," Travis said to me. "Gina has excellent taste," he assured the men behind the counter.

Our *Tea Sommelier* went on about equatorial regions and fair trade and first blushes, while the other wheeled a ladder across the shelves, climbed up and down, and held canisters under my nose. Told me to breathe deeply: brandied-pear honeybush, smoky lapsang souchong.

"Got any mint?" I asked, because it was probably cheap, and I was going to need a cup to soothe my stomach. I looked down. The floor was so highly polished I could see up my own skirt. I crossed my legs.

The experts were disappointed. "Peppermint, spearmint, wintergreen chill, or Moroccan mint?" the guy on the ladder asked.

"Give me the Moroccan."

He brightened a little. "Excellent choice!"

That meant I'd chosen the most expensive option. I do have a knack.

"I'll have the same." Travis smirked at me. This was what he wanted, to see me sweat over money. He pulled out his wallet and leafed through the bills. "How much?" he asked.

"Eighty-five."

Travis looked up from his wallet. "Dollars?"

"Yes, sir, for a pound. Fifty for a half pound." The guy sniffed, as if having to vocalize dollar amounts was distasteful.

"Give me a half pound," I said, and surrendered my Visa.

Travis set his jaw. "I'll take a pound."

And then it was air kisses and *see you around* for Travis and I. He got in his Beemer and I walked to the SkyTrain station, a fifty-dollar bag of mint tea in my hand. Feeling like it was all very appropriate.

* * *

I was told to come back to the courthouse in November, and it's the twenty-ninth. I'm lost. Travis did most of the navigation through the building the first time; I just followed. We haven't exchanged a word since. I drank the last cup of Moroccan mint tea this morning.

City blocks of heavy-tread carpet and plastic plants. Rows of doors with little brass signs. In front of room #228, a man in a suit speaks loudly to another man, who translates to a lawyer. Looks like a lawyer, anyway. Everybody's throwing their arms around and sweating. A woman right out of the movies sits nearby: red lips, little hat, navy stilettos.

She has a trench coat folded over one arm. She and her lawyer say nothing, just smile at each other. This is a divorce, and she's winning.

I'm in jeans and flats. My head has that 'too many coffees' feeling.

Acres of polished wood counters, each with a number and a bell. Each cardigan-clad counter guardian sighs with relief when I pass them by. To the left, forty-one. To the right, forty-two. Mister forty-three returns my stare, fluorescent light gleaming off his bald spot.

I read off the ten-digit identification number scrawled on my palm, sweating over what this step could possibly involve: money, bloodwork, paperwork that I've undoubtedly lost? He types the number into the computer and says "Oh, this is done."

"Done?"

"Yep, done ages ago."

"So there's nothing more for me to do?"

He leans forward, lets the corner of his mouth twitch upward.

"Nope. You're divorced." He rubber stamps a piece of paper, hard. Hands it to me.

"Thank you," I say, though I'm not feeling thankful. I feel like a thirty-year-old divorcee which, technically, is what I am. Some girl who reached the end of her rom-com before the part where she gets her groove back. Fuck.

I could get a drink or do something celebratory, but it's not even ten o'clock. People talk about having divorce parties. But those people have social groups. All of our friends were Travis's friends. I think of the woman in room #228; she's probably scoring the Bentley and the Mediterranean villa right now.

The courthouse is only a few blocks away from the shopping district. There are long lineups on the streets in front of the malls; I'd forgotten about Canadian Black Friday. Hunched men in heavy coats rub their pink hands together. At the door to Holt Renfrew, slim women in stretch pants limber up, venti coffees in hand.

"Gina!" a voice calls out. Someone down the line is waving at me. Claire. She's married to one of Travis's college friends. "Thank god you're back," she says loudly, eyes darting to the line behind her. "How far away was that washroom?" She pulls me close. "If they think you're cutting in line they'll skin you alive."

"Thanks for saving my spot," I say. The girls behind me narrow their eyes to slits, but they probably figure I'm not after anything in their size anyway. It's hard to eat right and exercise with a full-time desk job.

"I've been wanting to look you up since the split." She squeezes my arm. "My split, I mean."

"You too?" I show her the stamped certificate. "I just finished."

"Hey," she says, "I know I wasn't there for you."

I shrug. She wasn't, nobody was. I'd just assumed that was what happened to women who had affairs.

"But now we can hang out." She hugs me and touches a cold cheek to mine. Behind her, couples pour out of the mall. Red-faced and tousled, shopping bags in hand. Triumphant grins.

"I could use some new shoes," I say. "For work." Claire nods.

They're only letting in so many people at a time, which is supposed to keep shoppers from trampling each other. Claire's been in line since seven, but we don't hit the front until noon. We're shuffled out of the cold, but not quite into the store. The mall air smells like sweat, Calvin Klein cologne, and rubber. A couple of frazzled security guards try to look imposing. From what we can see, the place looks pretty ransacked: empty shelves, toppled racks.

Claire frowns. "I hope they left some for us."

A woman walks past, arms loaded with bags. "God, there was like, nothing left," she complains into her phone.

A shriek comes from down the line. *Oh my god you guys, my sister's in there, and she says everything's gone!* People start shoving. Then we're moving. And then, Claire, the security guards, and I are swept from behind in a rush of cold, pissed off, ultra-caffeinated shoppers.

"Woah, woah, woah," I shout at the girl behind me with her palms pressed against my kidneys. She doesn't let up. A couple of store employees hold up their arms, but it's like trying to stop an avalanche with a Swarovski crystal-studded shovel. Somebody steps on my shoe and tears it right off my foot. No time to look back. No sign of Claire.

The wave recedes by the time we hit DKNY, but now it's shoulder to shoulder. I look down at my stockinged foot. Those flats were my favourite. I climb onto a mannequin platform and look out over the floor. There it is, up the second floor escalator. Women's shoes.

An oversized, leather purse hits me in the chest the moment I step off the mannequin platform. The price tag says seven hundred dollars, slashed to fifty, but it's wrenched from my hands before I have time to consider it. At the bottom of the escalators, a security guard ministers to a woman with a cut on her forehead. She refuses to let go of her Estée Lauder gift pack to take the bottle of water he's offering. "Just call my husband," she says, over and over.

I look up at the second floor. I'm not going to make it up there. And if I do, what if there's nothing left for me?

Then there's a hand on my shoulder and it's Claire. "Come on," she says. "Let's do this."

Each step is a battle, especially with one bare foot, but we're committed now. I keep my head up, elbows out. There's so much pushing and shoving, but if I get sucked into the aggression, I'll lose valuable energy. Stay focused. Damn, should've brought a PowerBar. Claire squeezes my arm, but my breathing gets ragged because it's overwhelming.

"Bitch, we got this," she says. "Westside ex-wives."

"Westside ex-wives," I gasp back at her. Somebody pulls at my hair but I don't dare look behind me. At least security stopped the escalators. When I was younger I used to look at the green light coming up from between the cracks and worry about getting sucked under. Mall basements filled with the mangled bones of women. Women who died alone, while their husbands circled the car outside.

The crush finally spills out onto the second floor, and I can breathe again. God, women's shoes is apocalyptic: piles of discards, boxes, orphaned designer pumps lined up like bowling shoes. But we made it. After all that, I deserve some stilettos. But first, I need flats.

At the checkout, a teenaged salesgirl is taking selfies in front of the carnage. She sucks in her cheeks and pouts so it looks like she's dismayed and gorgeous at the same time. I'll never be that young and beautiful and skinny again. Oh well. Shoes.

Claire digs through box after box of black leather boots. "When this is over," she says, "let's get a coffee."

"Tea," I say. "I know this place."

Baby Boomer

Greg hears dishes hit the wall upstairs. So often now, he can tell the difference between a shattering dinner plate and a saucer. He hears the word *bitch* screamed at his daughter—his only child—sweet Danica. So he takes action. Pulls himself up off the couch, where he and Manon have been watching *Judge Judy*. Makes for the front door.

Manon silences Judy with a press of a button. "Listen to them up there," she growls. "Do something!"

"I'm going for a walk," he tells his wife. Mama bear.

"You're going garbage collecting." Creases around her eyes. She's lost weight. Looks like a deflated foil balloon in her silver tracksuit.

There are latex gloves and garbage bags waiting at the door. "Recycling," Greg says.

"Greg," she says. "It's only a matter of time before he stops throwing dishes and starts throwing punches."

Greg tingles a little at the thought, but he meets Manon's gaze with a smile. He knows Travis won't get violent. He knows Travis's type, all bark and no bite. A goddamn coward.

Upstairs, a tin coffee cup ricochets—at least those are built to last. Greg needs some air. The suite is small and cramped with his books, and the furniture Manon refused to part with when they moved downstairs. Credenzas full of bone china, saved for Dani. Dusty French colonial couches that smell like wax polish. Stifling in the humidity.

"Catch ya later." He gives her the finger guns, but she doesn't return them. Puts the latex gloves in his pocket.

Manon turns the sound on again. "Judy'd stick it to that little shit," she says.

It's been three years since Travis and Danica moved into the suite upstairs. A year before that, they were married. Danica was twenty-five, Travis twenty-seven. Not too young, Greg thought. Old enough for Dani to make her own decisions, whether he was onboard or not. Naturally, Manon disagreed.

"He's a bum, and Dani's blind!" she declared at the rehearsal dinner. "This relationship is doomed." Banged her fork on the table like a gavel.

Travis responded by throwing a pitcher of sangria at the wall. Greg remembers Dani, drips of wine trickling down her pretty freckled nose. Little pieces of nectarine stuck in the long brown hair she'd spent hours curling and twisting into an elaborate hairstyle. The smile never left her face as she rose from the table and retreated to the washroom.

Greg slipped the waiter a twenty to clean up the mess, then waited for Dani outside the washroom. "Honey, are you okay?"

"A little sticky," she said. "Good thing I chose the burgundy sundress!"

Greg brushed a piece of strawberry off his daughter's shoulder. "You're sure about this...about Travis?"

"He had it rough growing up." She kissed Greg on the cheek. "Not like me."

"Is that a reason to marry him?"

"Dad, I can help him."

Wisdom of the young, Greg thought. With a sigh.

When they got back to the table, an already skinny Travis had shrunk considerably. "Greg, man, this isn't me." He pulled Dani onto his lap. Buried his face in her neck, like a kid.

"Let's hope not," Greg said. Manon rolled her eyes.

So it happened: service at the Quay and photos at Queen's Park. The big magnolias in full bloom. Greg and Manon have one of the wedding photos on the mantel, next to Dani's high school diploma. Travis's family hadn't made it out from Toronto. Greg offered to pay the airfare, since it meant something to Dani, but Travis refused. He said they'd never make the trip for him.

Travis is stomping through the front yard toward Danica's car. Unwashed and unshaven, some kind of movie star look Greg doesn't understand. When he sees Greg, he's all smiles.

"Aw, hiya Greg! Sorry about the yelling. I guess I got a little carried away." He feigns a look of remorse. "Dani's bitchin' really gets under my skin sometimes, kinda like you and Manon, hey?"

"Not really," Greg says, noticing a large new tattoo of a shark on Travis's arm. "How's the job search going?"

Travis's grin evaporates. "Christ, you sound just like her." He gets into Danica's car and screeches the tires as he drives off. The smell of burned rubber hangs thick in the air.

Travis lost his job as a roofer six months after the wedding. He said he was injured, but Workers' Compensation wouldn't honour the claim. They said there wasn't enough proof. Greg certainly hadn't seen any. A few months later, Danica left the nursing program at the University of British Columbia to get a job as a waitress.

"Just until we get back on our feet, Dad," she told Greg.

Three years ago. Try as he might, there was nothing Greg could say to change Danica's mind.

When he really thought about it—how useless he was in the face of Travis's caveman rage—Greg wanted to throw something, too. But anger accomplishes nothing. So, Greg started his recycling campaign. He would get Danica back into nursing school and get rid of Travis. But he needed more money. He'd made a reasonable living teaching at the community college, but money had been tight since his retirement.

The kitchen manager at the college was happy to let him pick up the empties after school functions. Sometimes several garbage bags full. He combed the alleys six days a week, through Queen's Park and deep into Sapperton on the other side of the highway. Manon would die if she found out how extensive the recycling operation actually was, but a few times a month he'd even take the car into Vancouver and fill it with empties from the trade conventions at BC Place. It was a full-time job, but his generation had never been afraid of hard work.

Not like Travis, and his whole damn generation. Millennials. What the heck happened?

Tonight, Greg takes a route all the way up Seventh. Crosses through alleys to catch the neighbourhood parks with bins that are only emptied once a week. Some of the big family picnics wrap up their empties and leave them next to the cans. This makes his job easier.

First stop is the back end of Queen's Park. Just past the picnic tables, there's a spot where a bunch of old cedars stand in a circle, and the air always feels a little cooler. Greg stops and inhales. He used to do this circuit in the morning, because it was peaceful and he could be back home before Manon even woke up. But lately he's been running into other recyclers. Chinese grandmothers who smile and nod at him, with no urgency in their movement. Sometimes one of those guys with the shopping carts. A switch to evenings seems to have eliminated the awkwardness of competition. Greg pulls on the gloves and opens bin after bin, taking a few swoops through the top level of garbage, careful in case of anything sharp. Pulls out the empties with an efficiency that might make sorting through the trash seem natural to anyone passing by.

Next up is a little park where he and Manon took Dani when she was a kid. It used to have a zipline that ran from a tree fort all the way across to the other side of the park, until the city deemed it too dangerous for kids. Now it's just a couple of picnic tables and a "neighbourhood approved" safety swing set. No wonder kids got soft. Greg moves a couple of greasy buckets of discarded KFC and finds a two-litre Diet Coke bottle.

It's dark by the time Greg hits his last stop, a little park on Trafalgar with Japanese gardens and a duck pond. He walks over the stepping stones—almost indiscernible in the dark. Dani told him she's seen koi in the pond, but Greg's never seen anything but murk. Tonight he sees the glint of an empty Dr. Pepper can, but it's out of his reach.

By the time Greg gave his stockbroker a call two years ago, he had collected a thousand dollars in empties. He cashed in a GIC, and invested two thousand in Galena Ventures, a mining company that would pay off big if their new dig was successful. And it was. Six months later, Greg had five thousand, which he invested in a tech company in California. Fourteen months later he sold high, put five thousand in a savings account with Danica's name on it, and reinvested the rest. He could have stopped collecting empties, but he didn't. Playing the market is risky, and things can go south in a hurry. But they didn't. Manon had no idea about the money. He anticipated the look on her face when he told her he had enough saved to solve all their problems. Maybe they could take a vacation. They used to go walking through the neighbourhood together, before the kids moved in, but she rarely leaves the house now.

Wednesday night family dinner. Manon is carving the chicken like it's an adversary. "He's still parading around the neighbourhood like some kind of vagrant!" Manon points the carving knife at Greg. She's got on the gold tracksuit tonight, which at least gives her a healthy glow.

"Yeah, Greg, have some self-respect, man!" Travis combs his hair with his fingers and reaches across the table. "I've been unemployed for months now."

"Thirty-six months." Greg passes him the potatoes.

"Whatever, you don't see me digging through the trash." Travis stuffs another mouthful of chicken into his maw and reclines in his chair. He's clearly relieved not to be at the receiving end of Manon's fury for once.

"I don't think there's anything wrong with it," Danica says and squeezes Greg's shoulder as she gets up to clear the table.

"No, leave that to me," Manon says, swatting at her daughter. "Just get *him* out of here before he settles on the couch."

"I heard that." Travis bangs open the door to the upstairs suite as he leaves. "Comin', Dani?"

"Coming." Danica watches Travis leave. She starts loading the dishwasher.

"Dani, I'll do it later. *CSI* is on." Manon lifts up the couch cushions, looking for the remote.

Danica glances upstairs. "You watch *CSI*? I thought you hated that cop stuff."

"It's interesting. All the different ways they can trace a crime back to someone."

"Your mother's become a regular sleuth," Greg says. "She must have half a dozen Agatha Christie movies out from the library. She'd be the one to talk to if anyone turned up stiff." He grabs two garbage bags. "How about we go for a little recycling walk, Dani?" he asks. "I got you a pair of gloves so you don't mess your nails."

She smiles. "I haven't had a manicure in—"

"—Thirty-six months?" Greg says. When Danica smiles, he sees a grubby six-year-old digging up worms for their annual trip to Trout Creek. He sees a graceful twelve-year-old learning crosscuts at the rink and waving at him in the stands. And he also sees the future: Danica at her convocation, posing for a picture next to the rhododendrons with him and Manon. No Travis. He'll be long gone by then.

"We'll do the alleys; everyone will have their blue boxes out." Greg hands Danica a bag.

She smiles. "Okay, Dad."

There's a peekaboo view of the Fraser River from the front yard. It looks like mercury from a distance. The sky's full of pink sunset, but it's muggy again.

"Dad, can I ask you something?"

"Sure." Greg's cell phone buzzes—it's a text from his broker. Time to sell InfoTech.

"Was Mom always so ... aggressive? Like, before you had me?"

"I think of it as passionate." Greg shoves the phone in his back pocket.

"Did you ever worry that it wouldn't work out between you?"

"I sure didn't," Greg says. "Worrying solves nothing. No problem is unsolvable, but you gotta take action, cupcake."

Danica leans over the neighbour's blue bin. "Smiths must have had a party."

"Everything okay, Dani?" Greg asks.

Her head drops a little for a second, and she pulls herself up to face him. "Dad, I think I've made a mistake."

"What do you mean?"

"A bad mistake. A big one." She puts a hand on her belly. "When I really think about it, he's the last guy I want to raise my kid."

"Oops." A bottle of white Zinfandel escapes Greg's grasp and rolls under the Smiths' car. "Oops, oops, oops. Have you told your mother?"

Greg tells himself that twelve thousand is enough. Twelve thousand is a lot. He calls his broker, starts the wheels in motion. He can keep two thousand for Danica and offer Travis the rest to get out. Forever. If Travis gets wise and asks for more, he can have it. Danica won't go back to school for a few years now anyway. The money won't be available right away, but Greg can arrange some kind of payment plan with Travis. He'll have to.

When Greg gets off the phone, he hears doors slamming upstairs. But this time, his daughter is doing the yelling. Maybe he should have told her about his plan, but if Danica can get rid of Travis of her own volition, everyone will benefit. That's not greed, it's logic. Twelve thousand is a lot of money. Greg and Manon could take that vacation.

"I'm going up there." Manon has been pacing like a puma since Danica told her the news.

"Don't you think it's best if—"

"—I think it's best if I protect my pregnant daughter from that piece of shit," Manon hisses. She flies through the door to the upstairs suite, and Greg keeps his mouth shut. His plan has been carried out seamlessly up to now; he can't let emotion get the better of him. But he can feel the beginnings: hot forehead, a knot in his stomach, shortness of breath. He shuffles some tax papers around on his desk. Checks his phone. Now all three of them are up there yelling. He knows Travis. Travis will blow off some steam, and run away somewhere for the night. Then Greg can explain to his family how he is going to make everything better.

"Greg!" Manon's voice booms from upstairs, but there's something funny.

And then Travis's voice. "Bitch. He hates you as much as I do!"

"Jesus." Greg takes his phone out and dials 911. The neighbours are going to talk.

"Greg!" The fear in Manon's voice is obvious now.

Greg stands and heads upstairs.

He hasn't been in the upstairs suite since he painted the bathtub for Dani last Christmas. There's a hole in the hallway wall. Burn marks in the carpet, a cigarette ground into one of them. An overturned Texas mickey of Bacardi rum is rapidly spilling its contents onto the floor. Manon calls for him again, as he picks up one of Dani's old track-and-field trophies from the mantelpiece. Marble, with a gold-painted pole vaulter on top.

Dani is sprawled on the floor under the kitchen table—the same ratty Arborite table she grew up eating breakfast at. Her nose is bloody, eyes are closed. So. Greg was wrong about Travis. Manon was right. And now she's backed up into a corner of their old kitchen, eyes wide, nostrils flared. Travis is pressed against her, holding a broken beer bottle, his back to Greg. Manon's eyes flick over to Greg's and back to Travis.

Greg's movement is efficient. The base of the trophy hits Travis on the side of the head and splits the skin near his temple. Bright blood spurts out. He goes down without a sound. There's always a lot of blood in head injuries, Danica had told Greg once, when she was in nursing school.

The gold-painted pole vaulter lands at Manon's feet. She picks it up and looks at Greg, saucer-eyed.

"Wow," she says. "Wow."

"I saved some money," Greg burps out, bile rising in his throat. "I saved us." They're so close now. Greg can smell her sweat. He feels the hair on his neck bristle, the muscles in his thighs twitch. Then Danica groans, sweet Dani, and they both remember.

Chins and Elbows

A t 5:00 a.m., Lara and I are on the beach in Port Moody. The morning mist is sea salt and oil slick. Bleh. Cold waves slap the shore. It's a groggy, rubber boot clomp to the beat-up aluminum boat at the end of the dock. Lara volunteers with Nature's Little Helpers. Spawning season means it's time for an egg take in Mossom Creek.

"Triple Americano, black. Right?" Lara thrusts a travel mug at me. "It's good to see you." Behind her, a block of beige beach condos disappears into the fog.

"Do we have to kill the fish?" My hands warm around the mug. I won't tell her I've spent every day since I got home drinking decaf. Playing video games. Running a pale, thin elf warrior around a shimmery forest on her horse, killing monsters with a bow. Good versus evil is such a comfort sometimes.

"Oh god, no," Lara says. "Well, somebody does. We'll do other jobs." She worked with Nature's Little Helpers all summer, planting eelgrass along the shoreline, tramping around in the muck like a kid. She wrote me letters about it, each one an invitation to come back to the city. I'd intended to write her back.

The salmon enhancement crew are pony-tailed retirees who probably urban pole to the grocery store. Wheatgrass drinkers. Gulf Island beachfront owners. They hug Lara like old friends and look deep into my eyes when we shake hands. Weird. Seven of us crawl in, hunched over our hot drinks. Smell boat gas and fish guts.

A woman with a grass-fed complexion and long, white hair takes my hand in both of hers. "Carmen, I'm Diane. Thanks for coming out with us." She turns to Lara. "We'll meet the gals from Alouette Correctional at the river. It's a small crew today."

"That's fine, Carmen can do the work of ten inmates." Lara grins at me, flexes a lean bicep.

"Inmates?" I look at Lara, who looks at Diane.

"Didn't Lara tell you? They send us volunteers during spawning season." Diane is still holding my hand. She squeezes a little before she gives it back.

Up the Burrard Inlet in a tin can. Past freighters and trawlers and pleasure craft. Most years Vancouver stays green, but there's fresh powder on the mountain tops. When I left Prince George three weeks ago, snow was already dusting the downtown streets.

"How was the honey farm?" Lara asks. I have to lean in to hear her over the thrum of the outboard.

"It was hard labour. Heavy lifting. Sweeping dead bees into the drain every night," I say.

Her eyes narrow. "I thought they didn't hurt the bees."

"They were at the end of their productive cycle," I say, mimicking the beekeeper's gruff monotone. "Probably true, but it felt like killing off my co-workers."

"That's awful." Lara lowers her voice. "But you're clean now, right?"

"Three months clean." Saying it like that makes it seem like I've been dirty.

"I knew you'd do it," Lara says. The first hug in a long time is always all chins and elbows.

To everyone except Lara, my trip up north just looked like a weird working holiday. A detox centre would have made it official. So instead I bottled honey, swept and hosed the sticky cement floors clean at Sunny Valley Apiaries. The bee-keeper wasn't sure about me, half-blood city girl with skinny arms and gaunt cheeks. Shaking and sweating for the first few weeks, until the last of the meth had burned from my lymph. Crying over dead bees. Not surprisingly, there weren't a lot of other people who wanted the job, so I got to stay.

We watch an otter skim along the water, belly up. Something in his paws—looks like a plastic baby toy. He dips under, leaving his loot at the surface. Further up the inlet it's crab traps and prawn traps and fish nets. Then only water, shore, sky.

Alouette Correctional Centre is on the South Alouette River in Maple Ridge. Lara tells me they just built a new maximum-security wing, with little windows in each cell, above the bunks. The windows look out onto medium security, so the women can see how good their well-behaved cell sisters have it. If the maximum-security inmates behave, they can join in on community projects: horticulture or doggie daycare or this one, salmon enhancement.

As we approach the dock, Diane points to a tall First Nations woman smoking a cigarette on the shore. Just her and a grim-faced prison guard.

"I'd expected more, but maybe it's just as well," Diane says. "This is the first time we've had a violent offender." *Violent offender* gets finger quotes. The boat bumps against the dock as our wake catches up with us.

"I'm sure it's no biggie," Lara says. "Right, Carmen?"

"Sure." It's annoying to be included in this conversation, like I know anything about violent offenders. I suspect Lara's invited me on this trip as some kind of teachable moment—the ghost of Christmas future—and that's not fair. It's not like I was street hustling. And I stopped using of my own volition. A detox centre would have been cushier, but it might not have been punishment enough. Some mistakes have to be beaten out.

Diane gives the guard the two-handed squeeze. "This is Lucy," the guard says to us, nodding at her charge.

"Lucky," the woman stomps out a cigarette. She's wearing a numbered sweatsuit; powder-blue prison casual.

Diane hands her a jar with some water in the bottom. "I'll get you to keep your butts in there today, can't have the fish eating them." She turns back to us without waiting for an answer. "Let's go, everyone." Behind her, Lucky digs three butts out of the sand and drops them in the jar.

Climb from the boat to the back of a fisheries pickup, and knock through the brush. Compared to the coho, our trip upstream is efficient. After a lifetime in the ocean, they swim all the way back to the stream they were born in. I think about those nature shows with the bear in the river, gorging on fish that practically leap into his paw as they battle the current. Life's a bitch. Lara says the hatcheries have a much higher success rate than the fish who fend for themselves. She talks percentages as Lucky grips the tailgate with one hand, smokes with the other.

"This your job?" she asks me.

"Volunteer."

"I used to work downtown," she offers. "They call me Lucky 'cause I got busted around the time all my girlfriends went to the pig farm." Throws her head back and cackles. She's referring to a local farmer who was convicted for killing six women. Newspapers with photographs of missing women from the Downtown Eastside set the number at closer to fifty.

"That is lucky," I say, wondering what's so funny.

She looks me over: black hair, pale skin. "You're not an Indian."

"Métis."

"Half-bloods." She snorts. "You guys are the real nobodies."

I shrug—I'm not getting into this with a 'violent offender.' Lara frowns. The truck slips through skunk cabbage bogs, dark soil seasoned with pine needles. We duck to avoid the slap of low-hanging branches.

It's all wild rose and blackberry at the site, but no blooms this time of year. The last berries scavenged by bears. It doesn't look like the day is going to overcome its fishbowl start; there's a film over everything. The yellow rain-gear Diane passes out is a relief. She points to the river—a couple of the Mossom Creek guys are already stringing barrier nets at either end.

"This is station one. If you want to work in the river, put on the hip waders," Diane says. "Station two," she puts a bucket and some plastic bags on the picnic table. "Eggs and milt."

A volunteer emerges from the bushes with a decapitated coho. He pulls out a knife and sits at the table. One slit and carnelian-coloured eggs spill out of her belly.

"Sushi," Lucky says, and elbows me. "No, really, that's brain food right there." I move to the other side of the table, next to Lara.

"It's true," Diane says, "want some?"

"Nah, my brain's already wasted." Lucky laughs again. Everything's a big joke. She points to the fish bonkers Diane's unloaded from the truck. "I'll kill 'em."

"Station three, eh?" Diane glances at the guard, who shrugs.

Lucky sees this. "Come on, better the clubs than the knives, right?"

"It's no problem, Lucky," Diane says. "Lara?"

"Where do you want to be?" Lara asks me.

"As far away from Lucky as possible," I say, quiet. She nods. We pull on the hip waders.

"All right, Fishing Bear, show 'em how it's done," Lucky calls.

Diane, unsurprisingly, looks horrified. Half of me is horrified too, the other half kinda wants to laugh.

A few steps in and the river is pushing me around, a downstream shove over polished rocks. Now I'm in the way of progress. Around me, the coho are boiling. Their panic is tangible, but so is their resolve. Green ghosts shoot forward to snap at my calves, then scoot away. Encased in rubber, I still shrink from the contact.

A net proves useless; it bends and pulls when I dip into the current. I slip a little and swear under my breath. Sweat collects along my backbone.

"How do you do this?" I call to Lara, but she's too far away and the river drowns me out. Shouldn't have had that coffee; my heart is pounding. Tweaked. A feeling I've been trying to avoid. My legs stiffen and the force of the river increases, so I bend my knees. This can't be as bad as handling a hive full of bees for the first time, when they seem terrifying, before you realize that you're the Godzilla. I look down. The water is full of fish and all I have to do is reach in and grab one. Inhale, plunge a hand into the river and connect five fingers with a solid body. It fights and escapes. I swing the net around, tie it onto my back and try again, with both hands this time. I've never seen coho teeth, not sure how much damage they'd do. Lara watches for a sec, then she ditches her net and gets in there next to me.

Got one this time, right at the base of the tail. Heave and he's in my arms. I was not expecting this: hook-faced, black-lipped, red-bellied sea monster. One eye missing, ripped fins, torn skin. He's winding me—fights with more strength than seems possible from a body already half decomposed.

I hang on, restraining a Mossom Creek coho at the unforeseen end to his homecoming. Whispering hollow assurance: Lara's percentages, chances of increased fry survival. Don't be afraid. Do not fear that woman on the shore, your executioner. You won't meet death in your own river, what you were hoping for, I admit. But your DNA will be preserved, and that's what it's all about, really.

I don't know if he hears me. He stops fighting. Diane and the others are waiting on the shore with clubs and knives. Salmon enhancement. Nature's Little Calipers. I think about the bees at the end of their *productive life cycle*, but there's no time to think, really, before the river shoves me back towards Lucky. "C'mon, Fishing Bear!" She waves the fish bonker over her head and whoops like an Indian in a John Wayne western. Diane and the crew look at their feet.

"What a comedian," Lara says. But I'm laughing. I'm not sure if it's okay to laugh, but shit, I'm up to my thighs in pissed-off salmon.

"You're good at this," Lucky says when I give her the fish.

"I'll add it to my resume," I say.

"We'll go fishing when I get out," she says. "Could be five to ten still though, eh?" And again, even though I'm not quite sure it's okay, we share a laugh like a cigarette. Me in the river, her on the shore.

Lara gets the next one, a female. Flushed and grinning, she hands it off to Diane. Now some of the station-two volunteers are thinking that this fishing by hand is looking very primal and authentic, so they wade in with us. We pull salmon out of the river for hours. On the shore, humans cut eggs out of bellies, and squirt fish sperm into plastic bags, until it's time for hot drinks and peanut butter sandwiches.

"Don't you find this all a bit weird?" I ask Lucky over a hot chocolate, like we're chatting at Starbucks or something.

"What, the egg take? Like she says, it's better for the fish." Lucky nods her head at Lara, who looks vindicated. "It's still weird though."

After lunch, some of the volunteers gather around Diane. She dissects a coho for those who have never seen a fish from the inside. Lara and I have both seen a fish from the inside, but we join in anyway. Diane cuts the organs out one by one and piles them in a bloody clump: a purple heart, a liver, a swim bladder. When she cuts into the face, we all cringe a little. She gives Lara an eyeball and Lara balances it on the tip of her finger. Through the lens, Lara and I see the world upside down. River in the sky. Diane's bloody knife. The blackberry canes where Lucky's been hidden, since nobody wants to see the fish meet their end. She's still working away, fish after fish, soft thud against flesh. She says something I can't make out, and laughs. I can't see her, but through the fish eye, I think I see Lucky's upside-down laughter run down to the ground like honey. Absorb near the tree roots.

Grey Water

The ocean is still this morning. I can't even tell you what a relief that is. Those waves have been pounding away for days, maybe weeks, who the hell knows? Drowning out every thought, every sound. Those MP3 files you sent? Couldn't hear them. Tried to sit outside and listen, sun on my face, smashed remnants of a crab shell gathering flies beside me, but I got only the faintest inkling of your voice, the slightest rhythm of your poems. New poems! You're so prolific.

Who knows where my earbuds are. At the bottom of an unpacked box somewhere. I was holding the laptop up to my ear until thoughts of brain cancer washed away all other attempts at concentration. Your voice. That's what I really wanted to hear. Finally, I gave up on the romantic image of listening to you read poems while I gazed at the ocean and went inside. But I can hear the waves inside, too, just enough to bug me. Finally I got in the closet, laptop pressed against my ear again (screw cancer!) and could just make out your dulcet tones. Something about a train. And bugs. And sex, I think, though it's so hard to tell with you. Those fancy metaphors. At one point you mentioned trying to capture the (non-sexy) simplicity of an afternoon of midsummer rain. What I wouldn't give for some rain right now.

Amanda says the well could dry up at any time, and then what?

Amanda is a pain, even when she's not here. She texts every day asking if it's rained yet. Like she couldn't just Google it. She wants me to take three-minute showers to conserve water, but it's hard to wash everything in three minutes. Impossible, really. I do upper body on Monday and Friday and lower body on Wednesday and Saturday. That includes hair washing for upper body and leg shaving for lower body, and as you know I have very long hair and legs. Damn, that didn't sound as sexy as I wanted it to. Anyway, yeah, two showers in a row on weekends. You never know when you might get lucky—not that I'm looking—but hopefully it'd be on a Saturday, when my hair is reasonably clean and my legs are baby smooth. You'd like me on Saturday. You'd take the 5:20 ferry over, and walk from the terminal to the bookstore, and I'd pretend to be a little surprised that it was already 6:30, even though I'd have been waiting the whole day. We'd go to the pizza place after work and have a couple glasses of wine and an appy outside on the patio.

I'd have my nerd glasses on and my day-old hair up in a bun, kind of like a sexy librarian, only like a sexy bookseller. That's me. We'd leave the pizza place before it got too dark, since it's a long walk to the pub. Maybe I'll get a car someday. Somebody might pick us up, a good-hearted local, somebody I served at the bookstore that day. If not, we'd take the path that runs alongside the road. It's fine during the day, but a little creepy at night. There are no predators on the island. Just deer and raccoons. A local told me that the deer might take a run at me during rutting season but he might have been joking. Most of the time they're just running away. Or sometimes they hang out in the backyard and watch me, big watery Bambi eyes, tails twitching. Anyway, we might see some deer on the way to the pub. When we'd arrived, some islanders would be smoking a doobie outside, off in the trees a little. Neither of us would feel uncomfortable—it's the island!

I'd know the bartender, and he'd bring my martini over and shake your hand and ask you what you'd like. You'd be a little suspicious of how well he and I seem to know each other, and I'd reassure you that although he's quite handsome, and he does have a way with words, he's not my type. You are. There'd be a reggae band playing, and you'd remark that reggae seems appropriate for the island. You'd be right.

At one point, you'd pull something you'd written on the ferry out of your pocket and read it to me: a new poem or piece of flash fiction, or an excerpt from a novel-in-progress. I'd listen rapturously, chin cradled between my fingers, running my foot up and down your leg under the table. You wouldn't even stop to thank the bartender when he brought your beer, you'd be so into it. The bartender would nod approvingly and wink at me. Because we're friends, and I've told him all about you. And you're every bit as good in person as in my stories.

We'd have too many beers, and dance to the reggae band and whatever the deejay was playing afterwards, and we'd even end up outside smoking some weed with the locals before you'd wrap your arms around me and say "Let's go home," and I'd say, "It's a thirty-minute walk," and you'd say "I'll piggyback you."

And you would.

Damn.

It's probably not a great idea to do this to myself—imagine you here like this. It's comforting for a while, but it doesn't take long before I really start to feel sad. Making new friends isn't easy. I spend most days here at Amanda's house, reading, drinking wine. And looking across the Salish Sea at the ferry terminal in Tsawwassen. And wishing I could take a bath, which might seem like a strange thing to crave in this heat. Obviously, in a world of three-minute showers, baths are way, way out. Non-negotiable. And yet here I am, back from an hour-long walk home, hunched over my laptop, writing you, and looking across the hall at the tub. No friendly local stopped to offer me a ride. You weren't here to piggyback me. You're probably reading de Maupassant in a coffee shop on Commercial Drive, or something like that. *It is the lives we encounter that make life worth living.* De Maupassant said that. You're across the Salish Sea. I am here. It's harder to be here than you think. I know you said I looked relaxed last time we Skyped. I have to tell you a secret.

I *was* relaxed last time we Skyped. Because I'd had a bath. I know, I know! But it wasn't just a whim. I'd had a terrible day: yelling customers, screaming kids, a nasty pain behind my right eye that flared with every blink. When I got home, I dropped my laptop on the ground and smashed the corner of the LCD screen, cracked it, and that was just the last straw. I fell down on my knees and cried. Partly about the laptop and partly about my knees. Amanda has stone floors. I know that sounds melodramatic, but you don't know how stressful it's been. I was desperate to move home, to be with you. Since you refuse to come here to be with me.

I cried until there were no more tears, and then I poured myself a glass of wine. I sat out in the backyard, facing those bloody waves that never seem to stop smashing at the cliff, and one glass of wine turned into three. Those goddamn waves! I wanted still water, warm water. I wanted comfort. So I stomped upstairs and I did it. I drew a bath.

The well water has a lot of sulphur in it, so the bathroom smelled pretty rank, but Amanda's scented candles helped. I closed all the windows and put my poor, cracked laptop on the side of the tub and queued up all of the MP3s you've sent. The suite of poems, the novel excerpts, the seventy-five flash fiction stories based on *À la recherche du temps perdu* (which I've listened to dozens of times and really connect with, even though I've never read any Proust). You're so much smarter than me, so much more well-read. The candles smelled like cinnamon and cranberry, the water was steaming, and your voice was so buttery. When I shrugged off my bathrobe, a shiver of gooseflesh washed over me. My nipples hardened to buds. I imagined you standing there behind me, extending a hand to help me into the water. Your eyes on my body as it disappeared into the bubbles. I sat back, piling my hair up and tying it with an elastic, though some tendrils escaped and brushed my shoulders. You could have sat on the toilet and rubbed my feet, and recited all seventy-five stories. That's what I imagined, anyway. The cover of a romance novel, or an Amy Winehouse music video.

Wouldn't that be nice?

I sat in the water until it was nearly cold, to make sure I got the most use out of it. Surely no one could begrudge me one bath. Amanda that jerk, off frolicking in Iceland with some guy for the summer, all those beautiful blue volcanic hotsprings, all the sulphury hot water in the world.

But I'll tell you something else, and this I'm particularly proud of. I saved all the grey water—that's what you call it after you've soaked in it, in case you didn't know—and I used it to do things like water the dahlias in the garden, which Amanda has actually insisted I do, even though I'm supposed to be limiting myself to three-minute showers. Doesn't that seem kind of weird to you? Don't worry about yourself, but make sure a bunch of decorative plants in the front yard look their best. Make sure they get enough water. *The dahlias are more important than you.* That's kind of what she's saying, right? A bunch of goddamn flowers. I wasn't sure where Amanda keeps her buckets, so I used a bowl, which meant taking many trips up and down the stairs, but what else is there to do with all this time to my-self? I've used about half the water in the tub, so the rest is still sitting there. When it's gone, I'll reward myself with another bath.

* * *

Your letter hasn't arrived yet. I know it takes you awhile to write them, since you insist on using that complex pen and ink cursive. It's beautiful. The letters are masterpieces: exercises in shape and form, gentle thoughts, flowing words. But it takes forever, and sometimes I wish you'd apply the same quantity over quality value to personal interaction that you have for flash fiction. No offence, the quality of the flash fiction is still very high. I read a *Buzzfeed* article that said introverts have no time for small talk. But small talk has a purpose sometimes. It fills in the cracks between people. Maybe I'll get your letter tomorrow and feel bad for sniping at you. I'm sorry. It takes mail extra long to get to the island of course. Everything here is slower and more expensive. I thought the slower part would be nice. But damn, we're talking *really* slow.

Amanda called to check on the dahlias, can you believe that? She didn't ask how I was doing. The dahlias are fine, and the herbs are spectacular, they love a good drought. I was so annoyed at her when I got off the phone I decided to have another bath. But there was still some grey water left in the tub, not much, about two inches. I sponged out a little, into the stainless steel bowls, but then I gave up and just ran the damn water. Baths aren't really the cleanest endeavour anyway. Sitting in your own filth, sloughed skin, bacteria. I noticed that the sides of the tub were a little crusty, so I decided I'd completely empty it and clean it out after the bath. But I was so relaxed when I got out, I lay down on the bed and fell asleep. Now it's morning, and the water has been sitting in there all night, and I'm feeling really guilty. I'll take a bunch downstairs to the garden. It's Monday, upper body day. Which is good, because my hair is kind of gross after soaking in the tub. I should have tied it up. Not like there's anyone here to notice.

You know, I've seen photos of the drought situation in California. Comparison between now and ten years ago: reservoirs, riverbeds, lakes. Have you seen the photos? The situation looks pretty grim. But last time we visited, I remember people watering their lawns, boulevards with lush green grass, the long, long shower we took together the morning before we left. All the swimming pools we passed over on our flight home, little blue tiles crammed into an uncomfortable crush of stucco and asphalt. Water is everything, and they don't have much. Neither do we. The boulevards in Vancouver were green when I left. Are they still? Don't you feel guilty every time you take a drink?

* * *

You're not going to believe what happened. You won't believe it, you'll think I'm making it up, but I'm not, I swear. Yesterday when I got home from work, water was flowing from the ceiling. At first I didn't realize that it was coming from above. I thought the bottled-water dispenser was leaking when I realized my feet were wet, but then I looked up. Drip drip drip. The walls were soaked, and get this, the light fixtures were full. Bulbs encased in little frosted-glass fish bowls. Can you imagine if I'd turned on the lights?

Well, you know what I thought, of course. The bathtub. I never did get around to cleaning it, so it's still about three-quarters full. I thought maybe the weight had caused some kind of catastrophe upstairs. I slipped and bashed my knee on the way up, but I was so scared I barely noticed. The bathroom was fine though, so I ran over to Amanda's bathroom and the toilet was leaking. I've never even used that toilet. I had no idea what to do, so I went back downstairs and put pots under the worst spots, pulled towels out of the linen closet and wadded them up around the pots. I just kept thinking, "This could be used for the dahlias!" I went back up to the upstairs toilet and noticed that it was just running constantly, and I remembered something about jiggling the handle when that happens (I think it's in a Tom Waits song, right? *And the toilet's running, aww Christ, shake the handle.* Right? Am I losing it?). So that's what I did. Then I turned off the valves behind the toilet and that stopped the flooding part, but I still had to spend all evening mopping up the house, emptying the pots, and wringing the towels out—outside in the garden, of course. I wish it would fucking rain.

If you were here tonight, I'd light a fire in the wood stove. I know it's still too warm for fires. We'd open all the windows and doors. The sea would be still. Even with the night's breeze, it'd be sweltering, ridiculous to have a fire, so we'd get naked and lie on the cool stone floor. Any skin contact would be so uncomfortable, but you'd leave your hand on my belly, slick sweat bonding us, sticky drips pooling below the arch of my back. Every so often, I'd mop it up.

I think the overflowing toilet was a sign. I know it was. I've been wasteful, terribly, terribly wasteful. Like you, in Vancouver. You have boulevards, I have baths. We are terrible. I came to the island to write, and I haven't written a word, except to you. And you haven't written back. We don't actually care how things will turn out, do we? What's going to happen when the earth runs dry?

* * *

"I *vant* to be alone. I just *vaaaant* to be alone." Like Greta Garbo from that movie; what's the one? *Grand Hotel*. I've got a two-minute YouTube clip here. Garbo's keepers speaking desperately on the phone, looking for our heroine. Then, she suddenly appears in the foreground, tousled, a picture of malaise. The other characters—a concerned-looking matron and a grim, fatherly man—approach Garbo.

"Where've you been?" he demands.

And then Garbo says it. Breathes it. *I vant to be aloooone.* That's where the clip ends.

The island is long and skinny, and most houses are set away from the road, down long driveways. As a result, the roads seem empty. It's like the world just petered out quietly, no bombs, no zombies. Dry ferns along the shoulder, droopy evergreens, dry creek beds harbouring empty cigarette packages and yogurt containers. There's still the deer. I told you about them.

Sometimes, if I look at a deer for too long, I get weepy.

It still hasn't rained, but it's starting to cool off. Last week, on a misty road that was presenting me with a seriously pastoral farm landscape, I saw a snake. Just a garter snake, no big deal. I used to catch garters when I was a kid and freak the boys out with them. I loved the feel as they hugged my wrist, coiling themselves around it like they were claiming me.

I slowed down, but as I got closer, I saw it was half squashed. There was more carnage further along—a couple of flat lizards. The road was a reptile deathtrap. I looked away, at the horses in the fields, dehydrated green beans hanging from a lattice, sun diffusing onto Scotch broom. A foreign plant, and invasive, one of the locals told me. Still, it's pretty. I tried to take a photo to send you, but I couldn't do it justice. So I kept walking.

And then, yesterday, an eagle flew overhead and dropped a lizard on the ground right in front of me—yes, dropped it!—and it was still alive. Alive, but stunned. It was frozen in place on the road in front of me. Staring. I ran a finger across its mottled brown skin and it didn't move. I pulled out my phone and took a picture, not often you get the opportunity for such a close-up. But then I got worried. If it stayed put, eventually somebody was going to run over it. So I picked it up by the tail, crouching low to the ground in case it wiggled out of my grasp and fell again, but it didn't. I walked a long way into the woods, until I found a soft bed of moss—vibrant green and threaded with thin orange tendrils. There were a couple of clusters of unremarkable beige mushrooms growing nearby, and I could hear the gurgle of a stream, which was pretty amazing, since it still hasn't rained. I couldn't figure out how this place had avoided the drought; maybe an underground spring? But it seemed like a really nice place for a lizard to be. I took another photo, and when I looked at my phone, I realized that its skin wasn't brown, but quite a dramatic shade of purple. How had I not seen that? Maybe it changed when I put it on the moss?

I looked back down at the little guy, still suspended in time, and wondered if he really was still alive. Maybe he was dead. Maybe he was a she. Maybe something both other-worldly *and* organic was reaching out to me, trying to give me a message, and I was slapping its hands away like an idiot. Something magic. There have been other moments: eagles startled from cliffs, unexplained rock pilings. A tree with a big white equal sign painted on it, which was clearly a message to veer off the road and into the bushes. Before long I had bushwhacked my way into a grassy field. When I arrived (I can't explain how I knew that I'd arrived; at a certain point I just stopped walking), the first thing I felt was fear. Like I'd come to a sinister place, something out of a horror film. Like some guy in a hockey mask was waiting. But that instinct was wrong, not an instinct at all really. Maybe the opposite of an instinct. A powerful and lifelong misconception that I am not a part of nature. After I stood there for a while, I wanted to sing, I really wanted to sing, and even though I was worried someone might hear and think I was crazy, I suspected that that, too, was a powerful and lifelong misconception. Nobody is ever really paying attention to anyone but themselves. So I sang. I didn't have any real words to sing, but I'd been listening to some pretty schmaltzy new age music that morning, so I sang that. The whole thing may have been schmaltzy, but when the tiny songbirds started to sing along with me, I admit, it felt like a prayer.

Make no mistake, this place is magic. But magic can overwhelm you, it can make you sick. Disoriented. Twice now I've walked up to the bluffs on crisp mornings (still no rain) and looked out on Active Pass. There are other islands out there, which makes me feel better. Twice I've been overcome by gratitude for what the island is trying to give me—this new and complex perspective—and I've thanked it. And twice, at that very moment, I've heard the watery exhale of a whale. Surely such a thing should convince me of my place here, of my connection to the land. But it doesn't, and I think it's because you're not here. I leave the bluffs wondering if I've imagined the whole thing, if I'm losing it. Why can't we believe in these serendipitous moments with nature, or maybe even that nature might want to communicate with us? That it is constantly in communication with us. Lord knows we believe all kinds of other crazy shit.

* * *

You're going to think this is nuts. That is, IF you're still reading anything I'm sending you. I don't care. I've been thinking about those fucking dahlias, and you in the city with those big boulevards—big, *useless* boulevards—and I think, that's not what water is for. Not for keeping something so grotesquely unnecessary alive. Something that is constantly dying. Well, I guess we can't do anything about the dying part, we're ALL constantly dying, but some things are certainly more worthy of life than others. Dahlias are not worthy; they are big and showy and unnatural. Their heads grow so big, they'll fall right over if you don't tie them up. That's it, they actually grow themselves to death. But what about frogs? Eelgrass. Algae and moss and mould. Lichens!

Delicate things are suffering. I found three dead lizards around a dusty depression in the forest where there used to be a pond. They're desperate. I went looking for the spring I found a few weeks ago. The well's still not dry—I'm still the beneficiary of its gift, stagnant and sulphur-ish as it may be. And it's pretty bad. Amanda actually told me to bring home more of the bottled water we get delivered to the bookstore so I could avoid using the taps completely. I did bring some back, but I decided they'd do more good in the bathtub, where I've started something wonderful.

An ecosystem!

If you were here, I'd show you everything. The bio filter: bacteria, protozoa, and phytoplankton. You wouldn't be able to see those guys, of course, not without a microscope. Did you know that even though protozoa are single cells, some of them exhibit animal-like behaviour? Though they're not considered primitive animals, not anymore. But some of them hunt like predators, totally badass, I read it on Wikipedia. Anyway, I'm sure they're in there. Then there's the zooplankton. They are definitely animals—tiny and delicate. I'm not sure if I have any zooplankton yet— as you can imagine, it's hard to find lake water, and any- thing from the ocean would die in the tub. I'm thinking of ordering something online from an aquarium supply store. And then there are the snails (these were really hard to find, but worth it). The frogs were easy to find, but hard to catch. Now they're hard to keep confined to the tub, every time I open the bathroom door one or two jump out and I have to chase them down the hall. Rough-skinned newts, that's who

I'm looking for next, same as the guy that eagle dropped. Clearly that was a sign. And the leaking toilet. I see the connections now. You're probably shaking your head at this, but you haven't been here. With every day so quiet and clear, things start to work themselves out.

I'd work on the moss garden. You'd tend to the worms and insects with such care and attention, and together we'd foster the nitrogen cycle: waste to ammonia, to nitrates, to nutrition, to waste. Beautiful life, safe from everything, inside. It's small, of course. Just a bathtub. But once we got some fish in there, we'd have a humble food source. As soon as the rain started again, we'd never have to leave.

The Honey House

Monday morning. Al is lugging beehive boxes into the truck three at a time.

"Ever done any sailing, Ember?" This question isn't conversational; Al doesn't do conversation. I've been at the honey farm one week and I know this. I study him and try to formulate the least stupid response. All I can come up with is the truth. "Once. But I got so sea sick they had to take me home pretty quick."

"Figures." He reaches into the back pocket of his jeans and pulls out some packing twine. "I'll teach you a half hitch. You'll be making a lot of 'em today."

I nod. Al and I are going out to work with the bees. Claire, his wife and usual assistant, needs to make some deliveries to Vancouver.

"Over over, under, through. Easy." Al ties the knot with practiced precision while I race to keep up. He rolls his eyes when the knot comes apart in my hands. "Again," he says. He spends a good five minutes with me and my jute, repeating an endless cycle of *over, over, under and through*. When he finally throws up his hands, there are beads of sweat forming on his brow. "You'll get the hang of it. Get in the truck."

We're going to build bear fences. They've been wreaking

havoc on the hives in a few locations, looking for a free lunch. Just Al and me, alone for eight and a half hours. And the bees. Several thousand bees. Last week all I did was sweep the shop and scrape wax out of old hives, guiding any wayward bees out of the honey house with the respect I assumed they deserved.

Al and I drive a few kilometres out of town, towards Lower Madrona. Nearby, the alfalfa is tall and lush—a fodder crop for the town of Shelby's ranches. Al and Claire have hives set up at farms all over the valley. It's a mutually beneficial relationship—the bees get what they need to make honey, and they pollinate the crops.

Al parks the truck and the dust cloud catches up to us. Otherwise it's still, and already very warm. When I get out of the truck the first thing I notice is a deep vibration. Not in the ground, in my chest. Al points to several stacks of hive boxes, painted silver so they look like chest-high sky-scrapers, and I realize that it's the bees, humming like a sub-station. Above the hive boxes is a black cloud of frenzied motion. Hundreds of bees, weaving and circling each other like an airborne riot. "Is that a swarm?" I croak.

"Nah," Al throws me my beekeeper's suit. "A swarm's much bigger. And meaner."

A white painter's suit, ripped in a few places and patched with duct tape. Thin, white gloves. A netted bonnet, tied securely around my neck and upper body, and triple-checked for gaps. This is all that stands between me and the masses. Al, a tough guy, doesn't wear one. He keeps his little denim ensemble—a Canadian tuxedo I believe it's called—and works bare-handed. He gives me a hammer as big as my forearm, which he calls the ladies' hammer, and points to a pile of rebar. "You hammer those into the ground, and string wire around 'em," he says. "Over, over, under, through. Just like sailing."

Exactly like sailing. I wonder how the bees will enjoy a human pile driver just outside their door at nine-thirty in the morning. Al had said most of the bees would already be out working, but there are still plenty around. They whizz past my bonnet, on their way to drop off the tiny sacs of pollen they've collected on their back legs. Crawl all over each other at the tiny hive entrances.

Al cuts a swath around the hives with a weed-eater and sprays the area with herbicide so the tall grass won't short out the electric fence I'm about to build. When that's done, he checks the hives for bear damage.

The ladies' hammer is impossibly heavy. I need two hands to swing it, so I have to balance the rebar between my knees until it's secure in the ground. Luckily, the adrenaline rush I get when the first wave of annoyed bees arrives to investigate me provides some extra stamina. In a hive colony, there are different classes of bees. There's the queen and her handmaidens—nurse bees who watch the brood and take care of the injured. Drones are the male bees, the queen's love slaves. Of course there are the workers, who incidentally are all female. And the protectors, the hive guards. I assume that these are the ones checking me out, crawling on the netting that is three inches away from my face. One little buzzer lands right on the tip of the rebar, and I have to stop myself, mid-swing. God only knows what kind of hell will break loose it they smell the blood of their sistren. I wonder if they can sense fear, like dogs.

"Most of the time they're pretty docile," Al says, a psychopathic twinkle in his eye. "Sometimes you get a bad hive though. Bunch of assholes. Hopefully we won't find one of those."

"You're a butthole," I mutter, and keep hammering.

After the rebar is in place, Al sits in the back of the truck and heckles me while I tie the electric fence wire in place. As I fumble, *over, over under and through*, my bee entourage has increased—they want me out of there and I don't blame them. Then I feel a tickle on my chest. Against my skin.

Holy crap, there's a bee in there.

I swivel my head around to ask Al what I should do, but he's smoking in the cab of the truck, and what's the point, anyway? He'd probably spray me with herbicide. This morning Claire told me about an employee who'd had a couple of bees in his bonnet, and when he'd taken it off it, several more had come in for the kill. I can hear the bee buzzing confusedly inside my suit, and feel kind of sorry for it, but I have no choice. I hold my breath and mash her against my chest. Feel a new surge of adrenaline as the stinger pierces the skin. I gasp and scratch a little, hoping to dislodge it. It's been a long time since I've been stung, I hope I'm not a sweller.

Al's back. I can hear the grin in his voice. "Something wrong?"

I don't look at him. "Nope."

"At this rate," he says, "we'll be done the last fence by seven tonight."

"Fine," I say. The bee venom pumps through me, hardening my resolve. I feel a little light-headed, but that might just be fear.

After work I stop at the cold beer and wine, buy a single because that's all I need to get a buzz on. There's a park next to the pub, and as long as you're not rowdy, the police leave you alone to have a discreet drink at the picnic table. The can is wet from the ice bin the singles are kept in; I crack it and gulp the beer down until the cold makes my head hurt. Burp loudly. All this sweaty manual labour is making me act like a construction worker. Bees are feeding on the clover that grows in low tufts. I wonder if they're Claire and Al's bees, moonlighting from the alfalfa fields, mixing it up a little. Maybe I'll eat at the pub tonight. I kind of wish there was somebody waiting at my place with a pizza in the oven and another cold beer for me.

* * *

Tuesday morning, I can feel every muscle, every tendon in my shoulders, my legs, my back. Everything's fracked. The sting on my chest is a hard, red welt. Maybe I'll get the voice mail. Claire and Al will be annoyed, Donna, too. Maybe I'll get canned. Hopefully I'll get canned.

I don't get the voice mail. "If this is about yesterday, you don't have to worry," Claire says. "You did fine, but we've hired someone else to work with Al."

"Okay."

"See you soon."

"Okay," I say, to a dead receiver.

This is how adulting works, my mom would say. You have a bad day, and then you go back for another, hopefully less bad day. It's that hope that keeps you going back. And really, in a town like Shelby you don't have a lot of other options.

The first job I got out of high school was at Harris Drugs, as a cashier. It paid pretty well, but Mrs. Harris was an old bag and Mr. Harris liked to pat your bum whenever it was within reach. Then the Walmart opened on the other side of town, and everything local slowly went out of business, including Harris Drugs. They'd been around for thirty-three years, but I'd only been there for six months, so I was the first to go. After that, I worked at Walmart like everybody else. But working at Walmart is as creepy as people think it is. So I started asking around and somebody said the apiary was hiring. I didn't even know Shelby had an apiary.

"Ever worked on a farm? Any manual labour experience?" Claire asked me at the interview, eyebrow raised. "Then what makes you think you can do this job?"

"I'm a hard worker," I said, hoping it was true. "Tenacious."

A cat kneaded Claire's arm possessively and narrowed its eyes at me. Neither were convinced. "Why do you want to work here?" Claire asked.

"I need a new direction," I told her, eyes on the cat as if it was conducting the interview.

Claire made no attempt to hide her doubts, but she also admitted they were hard up for workers. I was hired on the spot.

"You'll need work boots," she said, glancing at my flip-flops. "And gloves."

"Check."

That was two weeks ago. The honey farm pays five bucks an hour more than Walmart, which means if I work hard enough, I can save some money.

The honey house is a two-storey corrugated-metal ware-house, painted yellow. It should look cheery, but time has done its thing, fading the paint to the same drab colour as the hills. The landscape is a disappointment too, not at all what a farm is supposed to look like—rolling green fields crisscrossed with irrigation sprinklers, cows, a big red barn. Barns and cows have nothing to do with bees, but I'd assumed that every farm had them. Happy Bee Honey is a long way uphill from the Madrona and the Goldstream, the two rivers that keep everything in the valley alive. Most people irrigate, but not Claire and Al. There's no point, since their hives are spread out at farms all over the valley. The actual Happy Bee property is just for bottling and storage, on five dry acres. Across from the house is a slouching, ancient honey stand, unused since the operation became big enough to supply grocery stores. A pile of dirt where the marmots live. It all looks like a doctor's office painting.

I pull my car up next to the house and crawl out. Claire and Al are already gone for the day, but Donna's here. A big cement slab serves as a centre point for the Happy Bee operation: honey house, tool shed, and a couple of other garage-like buildings with over-sized roll-up doors. There's the waxworks, as Claire calls it, a little super-heated shed where the beeswax is refined. A little further off, the outhouse.

As I grab my lunch from the car, Donna waves to me. Before I started here, I'd imagined a factory assembly line inside the honey house, like those old Bugs Bunny cartoons. The reality is not so exciting. One side of the building is filled with old rusty barrels marked *Argentina* and *China*. In the main room there's a beat-up table with a hot plate on it, a few boxy, weird-looking machines I haven't been introduced to, and two stainless steel tanks. The larger tank is huge, probably twelve feet long, and six high. It looks like the tanks you see on gasoline transport trucks. It's full of honey and always warm to the touch. The smaller tank is about four feet high, but it's suspended above a workbench.

It would take two people to wrap their arms all the way around it. There's plastic tubing running all over the ceiling, an elaborate system leading from a sump pump in the floor to the big tank. In the centre of it all, is Donna.

"You look nice," I say, hoping she won't razz me for being fifteen minutes late and moving like a geriatric.

Donna is big—big hair, big voice, big square hips crammed into cut-off sweats. She always smells like cigarettes. She pats her hair self-consciously, "You like it? The boy bought me a flat iron for Christmas, finally tried it out last night." She winks. "New guy starting tomorrow. First one in his pants wins."

I hadn't realized Donna is a single mom. "He's all yours," I offer. "Sex is the last thing on my mind lately."

"What is on your mind, my girl?" She called me that last week, too. I'm not sure if she's taken a shine to me or if she just calls everyone her girl.

"I dunno. Bees." I finger the sting on my chest and shudder. No more swelling, thank God.

Donna snorts. "The bees'll be the least of your worries here, Ember."

She shows me how to fill, seal, and pack little clay honey pots. We melt thick yellow beeswax and I pour it neatly around the top of the jar. Once the seal is dry, I wrap each pot in newspaper and pack them into boxes. When I'm a few pots in, I burn my finger on the hotplate. For some reason it really chokes me up. I mean, of course it hurts, like the bee sting and every muscle in my body, but I think I'm going to cry. I excuse myself and hide behind the employee outhouse, hot and waspy and stinking to high heaven, and let it out in gulps. I turn on the hose and spray myself in the face.

When I return, Donna looks at me, hard. "Nobody spends

that much time in the outhouse unless something's really wrong," she says. "Maybe it's allergies, your nose is all red."

"I'm just tired."

"You wanna go home?"

"Yes, but I'm not going to."

"Atta girl," she says. "Grab that box for me, the heat makes my back act up."

This is how life works. Points for endurance. When we take our lunch break, Donna gives me a smoke and I take it even though I quit last month. At the end of the day when we leave, Claire and Al are still out with the bees. Endurance.

* * *

Holy crap, the new guy is hot. Joe—that's his name. Joe. JOOOOOE. JoeJoeJoe.

He's over by the stacks of old hive boxes with Claire when I arrive. And he's shirtless. Claire introduces us with a look on her face that suggests she knows she's introducing me to a distraction. A beautiful, tan, muscly, smooth-skinned distraction.

Joe knows it too. "Amber?" he says, with a wink.

"Ember."

"Ember. Like a spark."

"Yee-ah." God. I'm an idiot.

"Come on, Joe," Claire rolls her eyes. "Put on a shirt and let's get going. You've got a lot to do before it rains."

"Bye, Ember," Joe says.

"Byeee." I watch them retreat. Claire's tight, economical strides and Joe's irreverent strut. He's not going to make it three days with Al. When they've gone, Al's old pickup leaving a dust cloud to settle on the gravel drive, I look at the crisp blue sky and wonder how it could possibly rain today.

But it does rain, clouds roll in, plump drops spot the cement and knock on the honey house roof. Rain is bittersweet: it keeps the wasps down and makes the employee outhouse smell like a wet fart. Cools the day, but weights it with a senseless lethargy. Donna and I open the big garage doors in an attempt to make the air move.

"So. Joe," I say.

"I know Joe," Donna says. "Didn't realize he was back in town. Joe's bad news."

"I've never seen him around," I say, wondering if she has her own agenda. She did use the flat iron again today.

"He's really bad news. His dad lives next door to me. Gangbanger."

"That's the first time I've ever heard anyone under sixty use that expression," I say.

"Well, whatever." She harrumphs, sliding a 15 kilo pail over to me. "Let's make creamed honey."

The rain also makes Donna's back act up, so this is another job that falls to me. "How did you ever get by before me?" I joke, but she's quiet, sets up a ladder next to the smaller stainless steel tank.

"Fill up the 15 kilo pail from the big tank, as much as you feel comfortable hauling up the ladder, then empty it into the little tank," she says.

"Really?" I moan, standing atop the ladder looking into the tank. It has propeller-like paddles on the inside, all shiny stainless steel. "That's going to take—"

"Forever," Donna growls. "I know. Get to work."

"Okay." I shrug. It's the first time she's spoken to me like that.

Donna reaches for her cigs, but I know better than to follow. After a few seconds, a thin trail of smoke wisps its way in from the door. She notices it and moves to an overhang farther away, by the tool shed. And then there's nothing but the soft splurp of honey pouring out of the big tank from the spigot, and the patter of fat drops on the tin roof.

It rains all day, but the heat remains, making the atmosphere thick and steamy. Donna's efforts with the flat iron have gone to waste. I wonder if Al and Joe will finish early. Claire told me they can't work when it's wet, since all the bees come back to the hive in the rain. But no, it's Joe's first day, so Al's probably making him wrestle bears or something. Donna shows me how to turn on the creamed honey mixer, to check to make sure it doesn't explode. Everything at a farm is a potential death trap.

* * *

The rain continues Thursday, so Al and Joe can't go out with the bees. Donna calls in and says her back's too bad to work, so I take her position bottling honey, and Claire shows Joe how to scrape old wax out of the hive boxes. It's a terrible job, but he makes it look easy—biceps rippling as a pile of dirty wax collects on the floor.

Claire and Al have deliveries. As she's leaving, she beckons me over to the door. "You're in charge," she says. "No goofing around."

"Sure, Claire." I try to look my most managerial. A bee comes out of nowhere and beans me on the forehead, bounces off, no sting, but I flail a little anyway.

"Still afraid of the bees? Ridiculous. Look." Claire steers me over to a windowsill where a couple of stray bees are languishing, and lets one crawl onto her hand. "Last thing they want to do is sting you. Last-case resort." She gently takes my hand and holds it next to hers, so the bee can climb on.

"Really?" I feel impossibly vulnerable, but I guess I'm not as vulnerable as the bee is crawling across my giant's hand. Its tiny eyes, tiny antennae, tiny thorax. It's fuzzy in places. Kind of cute.

"Really." Claire laughs with me, though I laugh softly because I'm still not totally cool with this. But then, in one swift motion, she reaches for the bee's head and crushes it between her thumb and forefinger.

I gasp and let the bee corpse fall to the ground. "Why did you do that?"

"See?" She's all business again. "It didn't sting you."

"Because you murdered it first!" I feel dramatic. But still.

"I was showing you how docile they are."

"Aren't they like, your employees?" Truly, truly idiotic, but I can't help myself.

"Ember," She says, deadpan. "There are plenty more where that came from."

I don't know how to answer that.

Back in the honey house, I check my reflection in the big stainless-steel honey tank in front of me. The curve of the tank makes my eyes look really far apart and my face look bloated. I suck in my cheeks and pull the lever on the tank. Warm, amber-coloured honey pours out the spigot into a two-litre plastic bucket. Fifty of these to do today, then the one-litres, then the clay pots with beeswax seals.

Joe sets down a stack of hive boxes with a thud and cracks his knuckles. I watch his warped reflection in the tank.

"I guess you could say I'm in a bit of a low, but I used to be big time," Joe says.

"Oh, really?"

"Yeah. I started off selling weed for my dad. He grows for the Angels." His abs are marvellous—as long as he's standing upright. I look away whenever he bends down, and they cascade over his chrome Hell on Wheels belt buckle and settle on his Levi's. He's definitely a little older than me, but not much, even though he seems to have been plucked out of Aerosmith. Every small town has a few guys like this. Shelby has quite a few.

"The Angels."

Joe snorts. "Yeah. Harleys? Leather jackets?"

"Of course," I say. "The Hells Angels." This is not a big deal, everyone here is used to seeing the long line of Harleys roll into town a few times a year. Checking crops or breaking kneecaps or whatever.

"Bingo!" Joe says. The putty knife he's using to scrape the hive box breaks in his hand and he cuts loose with a couple of f-bombs. "Don't they have any better tools than this?"

"In the shed, probably," I say, "but only Al has the key."

"Old Al's probably got a nice set in there." Joe glances toward the toolshed for a few seconds, and lights a cigarette. "Anyway. In a couple of months I was their top dealer, so they moved me up the ladder."

"Oh, really?" I wonder if Claire will be able to tell he's been smoking inside. "To what?"

"Lingerie." He smiles. "I sold Lingerie, to strippers mostly. Was damn good at it too." He looks me up and down. "What are ya, a size seven? Eight?"

"Oh." I cough. "I guess that's a pretty fertile market."

"Sure is," he says. "They gotta have something nice to take off."

He takes a long drag and looks skyward, adjusting his junk with the other hand. I put another bucket under the spigot and pull.

"I was living large, travelling around Vegas, drinking champagne and talkin' about g-strings with some of the hottest ladies in the world." His eyes narrow. "But the damn internet took off and girls could order stuff from China for half the price."

"That must have been hard to compete with."

"There's no competing with the Chinese." Joe grinds out his cigarette emphatically. "They're takin' over the world. Your kids'll be speakin' Chinese. You got any kids?"

"No!" I laugh.

"Married?"

"I'm only twenty-three!"

"Huh." He looks me over with an appraising eye. "Well, anyways, I was losin' money and I wanted out."

"So what happened?"

"Damn federales got me in Tijuana."

"What were you doing in Mexico?"

"Nothin', just picking up a prescription," he says. "Lemme' tell you though, Mexican prisons are every bit as bad as they say. No food, no bed, and nothing but a hole to piss in. I figured I was done for."

"Wow."

"Yeah, but here I am, and in two years I'll be back on top again. A guy I met on the inside is going to hook me up."

"But what about the internet?" I say.

"Not lingerie." He makes a weird thrusting motion with his body a few times, and looks annoyed at my confusion.

"Sex swings. Custom made. Something you can't find on the internet yet."

He starts to laugh, and I try to laugh along too, like mail order sex swings and Mexican prisons are downright hilarious, but he shakes his head and points at the floor. I look down and realize my bucket is full.

* * *

On Friday, Claire and Al have a surprise for me. They're standing in the front yard, side by side like *American Gothic*, only Claire is practically smiling. "Since you've done so well this week, you can cut the lawn this morning, and then you're done for the day," she says.

"Ever use one of these?" Al jerks a thumb in the direction of the ride-a-mower, and throws me an ancient pair of protective earmuffs.

"Well, no." I've never actually mowed any lawn. Ever. My dad always did the "manly" work around the house while I spent my time playing video games and trying to avoid cleaning the bathtub.

"Figures." Al enunciates carefully, as if I don't speak the language, while he explains the finer workings of the mower. Ignition, gas, blade release, gears. "For God's sake, don't hit any rocks, or you'll kill somebody," he barks as he turns the mower on. It's much louder than I expected. My shoulders crawl up towards my ears. The property is nearly all scrub, probably rocks everywhere. How the hell am I supposed to avoid them all?

"Well, off you go." That's it, dismissed, and he and Claire get in his truck. I guess Joe didn't show for work today. I wait until they're well down the driveway before I even get on the damn thing. My grandpa used to take me around on his mower when I was a kid, and I never lost any limbs. A guy I dated when I was a teenager used to take me four-wheeling in the spring. I'd sit behind him, arms around his waist, chin on his shoulder. I was in heaven.

I wonder if it's possible to flip a mower. It seems pretty stable. Like, entirely stable. Impossible to flip, in fact. I throw it into gear and lurch forward at about two kilometres an hour. Once I'm off the cement slab that the mower sits on, I lower the blade. The sound is like a jet engine. Dust flies up all around me, and I hear a couple of rocks go flying. I raise the blade, sneezing and trembling. Maybe I'll try the patch in front of the house first.

In sharp contrast to everything else, Claire and Al's front lawn is right out of *Better Homes and Gardens.* Not a rock in sight. I hack up a rhubarb (oops) and bump the fence a few times, but otherwise, I'm doing ok, though it takes me two hours. The sun is climbing in the sky, and I'm sweating like crazy. So much for getting off work early. When I get done, it's nearly four o'clock.

Back at the honey house, I turn the key in the ignition, and the mower doesn't shut off. I pull the key out. No dice. Put the key in. Pull it out. Shit.

There's no phone for employees to use and no cell phone reception. I stand there like a moron, staring at the mower with my mouth open, and try to formulate a plan. I suppose it will run out of gas eventually, but I can't leave it. What if it's still running when Claire and Al get home? The temperature is scorching, nearly forty degrees. What if it gets so hot, it explodes? Wildfires claiming half the Madrona Valley. All. My. Fault. I run down the driveway and out onto the street. Of course there's nobody around.

The nearest farm is about a quarter kilometre away. Two snarling pit bulls and a German shepherd meet me at the gate—so much for the neighbours. I turn on my heel and run back towards Claire and Al's. As I pound down the driveway, I hear the mower's engine sputter out.

Joe is standing over it, shaking his head. A mountain bike with a flat tire at his feet, shirt tucked into the back pocket of his Levi's.

He blows a lock of perfect hair from his eyes. "This'd be pretty easy to hot-wire. Hey, I was just coming up to see you, wanna buy a bike?" His eyes narrow. "Claire and Al aren't here, are they?"

"Joe," I say. "Thank you." I'm panting, tingling, exhausted and full of energy at the same time. I want to run behind the outhouse and bawl my eyes out. Or sit in the park and drink a dozen beers. Or something.

"You're welcome, Ember," he says. "Ember like a spark."

Ugh, that's so lame—eighties rom-com lame—and it's the second time he's used it. As he says it, he leans in slowly. I don't kiss him back, not exactly. More like swallow him. Tongue down his throat, my mouth so wide, we bump teeth. Put my hands on his chest and push him through the door to the waxworks and up against a wall. I feel it bend a little, then a lot, and for a second I imagine us breaking through and landing smack in the middle of the courtyard as Claire and Al pull up. That's so eighties rom-com too. But it doesn't happen. Instead I crawl up on the shed supports and hook my legs around them, surprised at my strength.

"Woah, Ember," he says, but I shut him up.

The heat is insane. The waxworks was a bad decision, with its thousand-degree furnace, but it's too late now. Joe closes his eyes—I keep mine open. His sweaty torso. His tousled hair. My breathless, steady grind, skinny ankles in work boots. The door is open and the bees are getting in, I can hear the buzz. Beyond Joe's chiselled shoulders, I see them drop when the heat gets too much for them. They'll stay on their backs with their legs twitching until they can't take it any more. Poor bees. Cooked to death by the heat, wondering where they took a wrong turn.

Read These Postcards in a Gonzo Journalist Voice

S tep on a plane and get off two days later. Shanghai stopover wins the day, like flying into a garage filled with exhaust. Freighters, evenly spaced, into brown forever. After we land, the plane just stops on the tarmac, nowhere near the terminal, as if it's also reached its limit of screaming infants and barfing passengers.

Zero degrees in Shanghai, but I'm dressed for dry-season Thailand. We are loaded on a bus and driven aimlessly around the airport for twenty minutes. I wish my sister were here so we could sing show tunes. We must have listened to *The Music Man* a thousand times when we were kids, *Jesus Christ Superstar*, twice that many. Now, the situation demands show tunes. Something to warm me up.

Finally, I get somewhere. The terminal. Teens with precision haircuts in pseudo-paramilitary dress answer all my questions with "no problem."

"Take my shoes off too?"

"No problem."

"Computer out of the bag?"

"No problem."

"Just put the nuke in the plastic bin then?" Hohoho. If my sister were here she'd tell me I'm not funny.

Deserted, dungeon-like hallways, and an escalator that spookily grinds to a halt as I arrive at its base, then resumes its grumpy ascent seconds later.

STOP WASTING ENERGY signs. Caps lock.

Sterilized water machines that play little tunes as they dispense my 25 ml portion into a plastic cup.

China, WTF?

* * *

If you've come to Thailand to drink, you may drink Hong Thong. I'm planning on drinking it. Specified only as "local Thai spirit." Sold in forty-ounce bottles for about 400 baht, which is half as much as most other booze. Bottles of Hong Thong are stored in milk crates in the sun, away from the other stuff, like maybe contagion is a worry. My boyfriend since last night—let's call him Julio—tries to buy one, and is asked whether he actually wants to buy gasoline. The woman says they fill the empty Hong Thong bottles with gas to sell to motorcycles.

"Any difference in taste?" he deadpans.

"No," she deadpans back. She's heard all the *farang* jokes. That's Thai for foreigner.

Turns out the actual Hong Thong is actually a few baht less than the gasoline. So we buy some shrimp chips.

This booze needs representation. A slogan dirty enough

for the days when paradise stinks. I'm thinking a bootyli-cious farang in a thong, leaning into a car window, shot from the back (of course) with some kind of slogan like "Hong Thong: Deliciously Cheap." I'm open to suggestions though. One liners aren't my forte.

* * *

Julio and I are staying together now. We decided to save a few bucks. Checked out of the Lipe Beach resort and into the Serene resort. Very Buddhist, in that staying there constantly reminds us that life is suffering. I could go on about the mould, the ants, the bar that's open twenty-four hours a day and only plays the same six songs, including an inane big-beat remix of "Signs" by the Five Man Electrical Band. But really, all I need to say are those three little words: *broken sewage line*. Like, right under our hut. Keep in mind, it's thirty-five degrees, and I've had food poisoning for the last forty-eight hours. Keep it in mind, but try not to picture it.

We told the owner of course. Three days ago. It's a full-moon party weekend and the whole island is booked solid, so there's no moving. Julio and I practiced grim acceptance until about ten minutes ago when I fucking blew my top. Then I pulled myself together—because public emotions are frowned upon here, even more than back home—and politely asked the owner what could be done. Over and over again. With a smile.

Now we are in a room above his "massage parlour" with no view, no bamboo ambiance, no mosquito net, and ABSOLUTELY NO FESTERING SHIT. And we are DELIRIOUSLY HAPPY.

Asia, I've got your number.

Watch out, motherfucker.

* * *

Very good day. We're out of the Serenity Now and back at the lovely Lipe Beach resort, where I'm greeted like an old friend by the staff. Thais love to welcome you back. I've been on Lipe nearly a month, and people at the resorts and restaurants wave and greet me when I walk down the street. "You're like a local now!" people say, which of course is utterly untrue, but it's the highest compliment an islander in any country can bestow on you.

I have my places. My people. There's the kebab guy—Greek, with a mohawk that's usually un-gelled, so it looks like a side-shave. He calls me princess and teases Julio because he always pays for the food. He says if women want equal rights, they should pay up. Julio told him he has the money because he has the pockets. We didn't tell him that all of the money is mine, because that wouldn't be as much fun, but the last time we bought some kebabs, I pulled the money out of my bikini. You can imagine the reception that got.

There's a gay bartender at a little coconut shack called the Zen Zone. His name's God. Yep. Loves classic trip-hop. We talk about Portishead and Massive Attack and Funki Porcini and drink Limoncello until we're slurring every word. I ask him if he knows how edgy he is, a gay bartender named God. He knows. He spent a lot of years on the Bud Light EXXXtreme deejay tour in the States. Julio doesn't drink there with me because he's a bit of a homophobe. Last night he went to the rasta bar and didn't come home.

* * *

I'm on a boat to the mainland. Fuck Julio.

* * *

A night out in Hua Hin, music in the centre of town. The Ex-Pat Jazz Band is shoved off the stage early to make room for a ceremony with a fifty-thousand baht novelty cheque. While they frantically collect their instruments, the singer of The Ex-Pat Jazz Band tells the audience he's never played to people who weren't dancing. Silence. Two hundred white people sitting in chairs with white seat covers. Behind them, a statue of Pone Kingpetch, Thai flyweight champion of the world in 1960.

The cheque is presented to a farang so tall he could be standing on the shoulders of a Thai. He's the leader of Biggles Big Band, all the way from Amsterdam. Last year they were rained out after playing only one song. He speaks Thai to polite applause. Asks if anyone is from the Netherlands, and most hands are raised. So he switches to Dutch.

Then it's time to play: Henry Mancini and Glenn Miller, and compositions by the king himself, ภูมิพลอดุลยเดช. Two pieces: "Blue Day" and "Hungry Man Blues." The king's composition is *tiiiight*.

Thais selling Heineken. Children and crippled Thai women selling roses. I shake my head, "No, kaa. Kob kun kaa, thank you."

I'm too drunk, again. If I had a cell phone, and he had a cell phone, I'd call Julio.

White lights over the heads of the Biggles Big Band, two hundred farangs, and the flyweight champion of the world. Kingpetch has one gloved hand raised in victory.

Thai lanterns in the canal that carries waste to the sea.

* * *

I worked all summer at a honey farm to save for this trip. By August, the hives were coming into the honey house faster than our little team could keep up with. Stacks on pallets every day, and yeah, the bees should have been coaxed out of the hives before they arrived at the honey house, but many weren't. And by many I mean hundreds. Bees everywhere, now exhausted or injured, crawling on the floor, the walls, the ceiling. Pieces of bees on the floor, having gone through the decapper, then the extractor, mixed with splintered wood and wax. At the end of the day, I swept them into piles, and down the drain. When I left that place, I didn't ever want another bee to die by my hand.

Pesticides are a way of life here, and I'm trying not to judge, since I'm only a visitor. And there are a lot of really gross bugs. But the bees. An open air hostel that gets sprayed for termites, and the bees fly through and are almost instantly incapacitated, but not killed. At night they are on the floor, sometimes one or two, sometimes a dozen. Twitching. Somebody sweeps them up.

Last night, I stepped on one. It surprised me how that indignant *why me?* feeling, a sense of having been bullied by nature, hurt more than the stinger itself.

* * *

Of course, every moment here is a "Thai" moment by default, as authentic as it gets. But I had expectations. There were marigolds strung into the stories of earnest young travellers, awarded prizes by journals and magazines for their gritty but delicate portrayal of Thai life.

Well, there's no shortage of grit here. But where the hell are the marigolds?

Then it's four in the morning and I'm banging away at the laptop and slapping at no-see-ums, and I hear the monks. Chanting? That's what it sounds like.

Pad over teak floors to the window. There's the call of cicadas and pre-dawn rooster zealots, and yes, definitely chanting, but no—this is wrong. I need a gauzy dress, and a clay mug of ginger tea in my hands. I need to be on the beach, or a breezy porch. But the air is thick and sultry—I can't hear the chanting from the porch and there's no beach for miles. So I'm catching my Buddha moment through grimy glass slats with nothing but cement crumble and jungle overgrowth in my view. The monks voices swell, and I have no idea what they're saying, but it's okay. It's only me here, in my underwear. Keep listening.

* * *

Teaching English in Chiang Mai in exchange for room and board. The kids probably think I'm weird, but it's because I love them, like, I'm really crazy about them. I can't stop smiling at them. It's got nothing to do with biological clocks. I don't want a kid of my own.

But these kids.

These kids with their polite *gooood mahhning teachuuh Ka-leeeee* and the way they let their little hand rest on my leg when they show me their drawings. Their weird, long-sleeved bathing attire with matching bathing caps. Thai modesty.

These kids take care of each other. Today a little boy is added to the class. His mother is Thai, his father French. The little boy looks more like me than the other kids, and he only speaks French, but that doesn't matter. My kids never leave his side. They touch him a lot, but it doesn't seem to bug him. The kids are all pretty touchy here, come to think of it. And smiley.

I don't know how to talk about smiles without getting all

cliché, but I'd heard there was something special about the Thais' smile, and I heard right. It's not just a routine tightening of the jaw—it's an event. Afterwards, you feel less lonely, if you remember to pay attention while it's happening. This isn't easy for me. I often forget to pay attention during hugs too. I have a friend back home who gets me into hug position, and then reminds me to pay attention to what is happening. Hugging is happening. He's a good friend.

For the first time in five months, it's raining.

* * *

The Songkran water festival scrubs even the most stubborn alleys clean. Hello Kitty mopeds dart around, and motorcycles roam the streets in tight packs. Passengers working rear squirtgunner, black hair plastered against knockoff Ray-Bans. Tinted-window pickup trucks cruise at parade speed, lean shirtless dudes in the back, with beach pails. These are the real high rollers of Songkran, kings of the alley. Taunting the poor saps on the street with nothing more than a garden hose.

"Hey you, stop!" A chubby guy holding a tiny squirt gun in one hand and an umbrella in the other barks at me. I move closer so the gun can reach me.

Dry season is over. Green smoothies at the stand on the corner for breakfast, and basil omelettes for dinner. Next time I pack up, it'll be to catch the overnight bus to Bangkok. Overnight flight to Shanghai. Morning flight to Vancouver, where spring is starting. I'll get home nearly before I've left.

Exotica

Melanie is mad, I can tell by the way she's picking at her nails. Really long nails, lilac coloured with little crystals. *Pick pick pick.* She has a new Coach purse in lilac; I was there when the UPS man delivered it yesterday. In the Yukon, you shop by mail. She has lilac throw cushions coming in the mail, too. She and Don have two cars and a nice duplex in Takini, up atop Two Mile Hill. A view of the city. "It's all about the view," Don had said, standing on their porch with a Scotch in his mitt. I don't get that. The Whitehorse view is all skinny trees and exfoliated hills. I guess you have to imagine Jack London in there somewhere, running around in a fur loincloth, even though Wikipedia says he wasn't actually up north for very long.

I shouldn't have had so many beers. Xander and I shouldn't have had so many beers at that old-timey northern bar this afternoon. Or was it this morning? Time is disappearing. Melanie said they wanted to hike tonight, in the midnight sun. Midnight Sunday hike on Mackintosh Mountain, where the Olympic cross-country skiers train. The pre-hike tailgate party at the base of the mountain was Xander's idea. He's an ideas man. My man. Bison burgers and wheat beer with orange slices (orange?).

"No lemons," Melanie says. "It's not always easy to get fresh citrus up here."

"Savages," Xander snarls. He spits into the barbecue.

Melanie's eyes widen. *Pick pick pick.*

* * *

Light all the time. The northern solstice is pulling the top off my skull and I feel like a New Age cliché. The motifs are ravens (raven lunatics!) and the ubiquitous light. Midnight sun in the coffee, and pushing through the blackout blinds. The smells are lavender oil on the six-hundred-thread-count pillowcase I lay my head on at "night," and pine in the air. Pine down at the footbridge over the green Yukon river. Still a tangle of current, even with the rapids blasted out. The trees are so scrawny here.

The colours are red roses on the sheets and green rivers in the waking hours, but the light is inescapable so where does that leave us? With magnets in our heads. Nodding toward the poles.

"You should go see the midnight dome," Don says. "No, really, you should go. The sun comes down and touches the horizon, and then it rises again."

The midnight dome is in Dawson City, eight hours from Whitehorse. When I lived up north, an eight-hour drive was no big deal. That was a long time ago, years before Melanie and Don had ever been to Whitehorse.

"I think we'll stick around," I say.

Melanie and Don look down at their fancy hiking shoes.

"So, ready to hike?" *Pick pick pick.* Melanie's going to have to get new crystals put on. She and I were good friends at university. But she's been up north for a long time.

"Hold on," I say. "One more round."

"You can drink while we walk," Don says. "I'm tired of waiting."

* * *

I feel like a New Age cliché because I want to talk about dreams, but what else is there to talk about in this sleep-wakefulness? My daytime self is nearly incoherent but my nighttime self is busy writing happy endings to stress dreams. The ones lucidity usually cuts off before the finale. Frantic packing for a flight I know I'll miss. But last night (or was it this morning?) I filled suitcases leisurely, in black-and-white comic-strip frames. Goodbyes in thought bubbles. Shook hands with my ex-husband, and flew away. To Xander. A happy anti-climax.

"How did you guys meet?" Melanie narrows her eyes at Xander. He's much younger than me.

"Poetry class," Xander says. Puts an orange slice in his mouth and gives her a citrus grin.

"That's cheesy!" Don laughs. He is much older than all of us.

Xander shrugs, spits out the rind. "Her husband caught us in bed. I was reading Rumi to her between thrusts. He had a dozen red roses and he threw them on the floor when he saw. 'Lovers in a Dangerous Time' was playing."

"Ha!" I say, wishing I had an irreverent cigarette to light. "The roses part is true."

* * *

There's a disc-golf course at the base of the mountain. Old

guys with silver ponytails and three wolf-moon T-shirts are smoking weed. They nod, we nod.

"There's the ten-kilometre World Cup trail," Don says. "That may be a bit much for you guys." He has short legs and a bit of a paunch. Face shaped like a pear. He's lost weight since the last time I saw him, at their wedding. It might be the gluten-free diet Melanie's got them on.

"Are you kidding?" I say. "Xander will carry me."

He burps. "That's right, honey."

"It's a black-diamond trail," Melanie says.

"Sure, on skis," I say. "Don't worry about us; just take us to the best view, Don."

He smirks, a little. "Okay."

Even when we start to climb and the beer makes me wheeze a little, I keep up. We have to keep moving or the mosquitos close in. They're much bigger up north, and they can latch on even in a stiff breeze. They bite along the hairline, on eyebrows, and easily right through denim. Bastards. The trails are wide and rolling, speckled with lupin and yarrow and some other tiny little pink flower Melanie can't identify.

"Do you find the solstice makes you a bit squirrely?" I ask her.

"Huh?" The corners of her mouth turn down. "No."

"Nothing? No funny dreams? No insomnia?"

"It's all the light," she says. "But it doesn't bother Don and I anymore."

Wildflowers and sunlight and dreams. There must be something else to talk about. "Unicorns?" I say aloud.

"What about them?" Melanie says.

"Nothing."

Up ahead, Don and Xander are not making man-conversation. They're not making any conversation at all.

* * *

Another dream from last night: free-running through a Moroccan hotel courtyard, so lithe I'm on strings. This dream is usually a chase scenario, set in a Toronto steel-and-glass venue of elevators trapped between floors. There's usually a bomb, or some spies chasing me. This time it's exotic: curved awnings and stone passageways, pink-flowered vines trail out of windows. I run for the feel of it, easily keeping ahead of unseen bad guys, and when I have my fill of movement and architecture, I stop. Then there's nothing left to do but walk into wakefulness. I'm laughing at how easy the end is, but it sounds like gasping when I open my eyes in Melanie and Don's guest room (sun!). Xander rolls an arm over me. "It's okay," he whispers. "Just a dream. It's okay." I realize how seldom I let dreams run their course, preferring a smash-cut into consciousness.

We come to a one-room cabin with a firepit out front. It's got a little wood stove inside as well. A couple of empty wine bottles. Someone's smoked an entire pack of Craven Ms, and butted out each one on the wall. Twenty black burn marks in a neat line, with an empty pack on the floor.

"Do you want to keep going?" Don asks.

I swat at my ankles. "I don't think this should be our final destination."

* * *

Melanie is bragging. "Don is the head of his department now, and they've asked him to chair the board."

"Congratulations," I say.

"What kind of board?" Xander asks.

Don pauses. "The Aboriginal Arts Advisory Board."

"Oh?" Xander says. "You're going to advise Aboriginals about how to make art?"

Xander's half Haida. Don isn't half anything, I don't think. He clears his throat. "It's not like that."

"No? What's it like?" Xander sounds dangerous, but I know he's joking. He loves to push a little.

Don meets Xander's gaze. "We help with grant money, organize shows."

"Don had to work hard to earn their respect," Melanie says.

"Whose respect? The Aboriginals?" Xander grins. "Good for him."

"Turn here." Don points to a marker sign painted on a canoe. The canoe is nailed to a tree. For the next few kilometres we're away from the view, into scrub forest. Xander and I walk a little farther ahead of Melanie and Don.

"Be nice," I say.

"These guys think they're a big deal, hey?"

"Maybe they think we think we're a big deal."

Xander pats me on the bum. "I hadn't thought of that."

"Me neither, honestly," I say. "Not until now."

"Is Xander mad?" Melanie asks, when Xander steps away to relieve himself. Don keeps walking.

"No," I tell her. I'm not sure what else to say.

"I like him," she offers, "he's very...playful."

"Yeah," I say.

"How are things since the divorce?" She leans in close. "Really?"

"That's what the therapist is for, I guess." I don't want to have this conversation now, not while the northern solstice is pulling the top off my skull and picking around—adding up numbers. But it's nice that she'd ask.

Xander rejoins us. "Where's Don?" he asks. "I need to let him off the hook."

"He's up ahead," Melanie says. She points up the path, but keeps her eyes on Xander.

"I'll run and catch up." Xander zigzags across the path, stiff arms, *Mission Impossible* style.

"He's so fit," Melanie says. "I'm kind of jealous."

"I'm jealous of your nails," I say. And it's true, I am, kind of. And the lilac cushions coming in the mail, even though I haven't seen them yet.

We walk along, quiet. The sun is as close as it's going to get to setting. "We're almost at the view," Melanie says. "You'll love it."

Last Call

S uicides. It's a job. Trev did two years as a telephone counsellor in Substances before they moved him here. Was it a promotion? Hard to say.

"The Panic Room" someone had dubbed Suicides years ago, back when the program was new. When there was tons of government money and every counsellor had a vacation allowance and a dental plan and a headset. "Don't Panic!" is scrawled in black Sharpie across a banner of dot matrix printer paper, which still hangs, forgotten, over the vending machines. Pseudo-healthy snacks—All Bran Bars, and Oatmeal To Go. Today, most of the counsellors refer to this department as "Last Call," but never when the team leaders are around.

"Always, always answer on the first ring." says Danya, Trev's new team leader in Suicides. Looks like a natural blonde, and a natural D-cup. Maybe bigger. A bit too chubbs to be truly hot. Everybody here eventually puts on a few. There's a company gym: a bunch of stationary bikes and *Sweatin' to the Oldies* VHS tapes, gathering dust. Cocaine keeps you thin; Trev knows this. Grabs a handful of his growing paunch.

Press 1 for help with alcohol or drugs.

"Never put someone on hold. That's different from

Substances." Danya winds her hair around a finger. Her nails are painted red. She's wearing red lipstick; her slow-motion lips form words.

"If you think you need help with something, wave your arms around; I'll come to you." She gives him a headset. Winks. "There's Timbits in the coffee room. Carrie brought 'em."

"Thanks," Trev says. *Timbutts*, he thinks as she walks away.

Here in Suicides, the curtains are always drawn. Yellow light filters lazily through dust and stale coffee air. Trev works graveyard. A half-dozen faces, illuminated like a campfire storyteller's by Reddit feeds. Or whatever's big on YouTube. Music is allowed, but it's hooked up to the phone system, so it shuts off when a call comes in. This makes for a weird, staccato soundtrack on busy days: Christmas, New Year's, and most of February. Trev used to sneak in his iPod, but he hardly notices now. Dark spots on the walls where motivational posters used to be. The kind you see at the dentist's office, a ruggedly handsome man atop a snow-capped mountain. *Success: Aim above the mark to hit the mark.* Ralph Waldo Emerson. Most of the posters have been stolen, more for the sport of it than anything. Unlike other departments, Suicides runs twenty-four hours, seven days a week. Right now, the time is three hours to Valentine's Day.

"You know saltwater taffy?" Carrie, who sits behind Trev, is leaning over his desk. She has a Hello Kitty pencil case and pictures of some beefcake with a crewcut on her cubicle walls. They're signed in the corner—*XOX Ken*—like he's some kind of rock star.

"Is that a band?" Trev deadpans. His cubicle is empty,

save a little Lego man he won at an office Christmas party. A scuba diver. He leans against Trev's phone, wearing a tiny respirator. A long way from the ocean.

"It's this, like, pastel-coloured candy." Carrie chews on the end of a pen. She smells like Calvin Klein and cigarette smoke. "When I was a kid, there was always a table at the grocery store that was loaded with it."

"You actually bought that shit?"

"I don't think anyone ever did." She laughs. "They probably still have the exact same candy from when I was a kid."

"Probably." Trev wonders if Carrie is the threesome type. She's got this kind of anime vibe. Japanese schoolgirl.

"I stole one from Safeway once. I ate it in bed after my parents had gone to sleep."

"Bad girl, huh?"

"It tasted like shit." Her cell phone rings. "Like plastic and red dye number 5. I'm craving some now though." She checks the number. "I have to take this." She presses a button on her desk phone to take her out of the incoming call queue.

It's mostly women in Suicides, which may seem logical, women being the more sensitive gender. But real sensitivity won't help you here. There are breakages. Tom from Substances in a permanent Xanax sleep. An ethernet cable pulled tight around the neck of Emily from Family Planning. There's therapy in the benefits plan, six visits per year. Employee retention is key. They'd paid for Trev's detox, thankfully. Then they transferred him here.

Trev checks his email, though he's not really sure who'd have sent him anything. He'd half-heartedly separated himself from all his "party friends" after detox. It hadn't taken long to dissuade them. The clean make the users feel guilty. He spent the next three weeks in his apartment, swaddled in polar fleece in a beanbag chair, willing himself to call *her*. She'd driven him to the centre. She'd called him every other day, but there was always some excuse not to come to the phone. So she stopped calling. When she changed her Facebook status to "single," he deleted her number from his phone and her name from his memory. He'd liked her though. She'd introduced him to raw oysters with horseradish, and taken him bungee jumping. She'd bought him a journal: leather-bound with a cord to keep it tied shut.

And she fucked like a porn star.

Press 2 for help with personal relationships.

Trev shifts restlessly against the bulge in his Levi's. Carrie is still on her cell phone, nodding solemnly. Danya is laughing with another girl that Trev hasn't met. The girl has pale skin and black hair; the same pixie haircut as his ex. Tattoo on her right forearm. A dead crow, its feet curled in a rigor mortis grip. He rises from his desk, a stick of gum in his mouth. Messes his hair. He's ready.

"Pretty slow tonight." Trev grins, but the tattoo girl's phone rings, as if on cue, and she waves him and Danya away.

"People are busy getting their expectations up," Danya says. "Tomorrow is when everything falls apart." She looks at her watch. "Two hours."

"Tick tick tick."

"Last year, this guy called in on his cell, from a bridge," Danya says. "I could hear the cars whizzing by in the background."

"Date didn't go so well?"

"Found his wife in bed with a chick." Danya rolls her eyes, "So cliché." She steers Trev towards the coffee room. "The creepy thing was, I heard more than one person yell 'Do it!' as they drove by."

"Creepy."

"Totes creepy." Danya bats her lashes at Trev, campy. "You got a girlfriend, handsome? Boyfriend?"

"I have a deep fryer."

Danya snorts. "It's hard to date when you're here. I'm always either working or sleeping."

"Or thinking about work, or daydreaming about sleep."

Danya hands Trev a cup of coffee and their fingers brush. "Or getting shitfaced."

"There's that."

The coffee room was the call centre's last attempt at optimism, decked out with leftover outdoor furniture from Expo 86, in pink and lime and aqua. A half-pillaged box of candy sits on the table next to the coffee pot. It's deep red and plushy, like you see in cartoons. Trev considers, but they all look like nut clusters. He likes the truffles. Danya takes three. Puts two back. Someone's playing Dean Martin over the shared music system. *Happy Valentine's week!!!* is written on the whiteboard.

This time last year, Trev had been at the Waldorf with *her* and some buddies from Substances. He'd done way too much blow and probably kissed someone he shouldn't have. She'd left him there.

"I shouldn't tell you this," Danya says. Her voice is husky. "But I have a two-six of Sailor Jerry in my office."

Trev's ready for this. "I'm giving my liver a break."

"You're gonna make me drink by myself?"

Trev shrugs. "No judgment here."

When they pass Carrie, she is crunched over in her cubicle, head in her lap. Danya's all over her. Mother hen.

"Bad call?" Trev asks, stupidly. Got to say something.

Carrie nods, her curls fall down over her knees. "It's Ken."

Danya blinks. "He called? Here?"

Carrie unfurls, raccoon-eyed. Holds up her cell phone. "He wants to break up with me!"

Trev checks his watch. "He's early."

Danya elbows him. "Carrie, you and Trev come with me to my office."

"Jus' gimme a sec." Carrie pulls out a compact and an eye-liner pencil. She's a trooper.

Danya's "office" is really just a cubicle with slightly higher walls. Portable plastic covered in tweed, somewhat separated from the front line. Middle management.

"You think it would be mostly girls calling on V-Day, but it's not." Danya is pouring hefty shots into Carrie's coffee cup. "Women are used to being fucked around. They have coping skills. It's the men who don't know how to process." She winks. "Sorry, Trev."

He shrugs. "You're probably right." His eyes are on tattoo girl. She's finished her call, so Dean Martin's voice is vamping through Suicides once again. He imagines her above him. Below him. From the back. Right now, she can be anything for him. The endless opportunity of the unknown.

Carrie sniffles a little. She's recovered herself pretty quickly. That's a skill you learn here, how to hold it in. The real trick is letting it out again later. Danya passes her a tissue.

"Has she been here long?" Trev nods in tattoo girl's direction.

"Nat? A few months." Danya looks from Nat to Trev and back again. "Might as well get her over here for happy hour too."

A few rum and Sprites—since Sprite is all that's left in the vending machine—and a round of shots. No one complains when Nat produces a bottle of tequila from her backpack. Trev's favourite. He needs some breathing space. Runs across the street to the Safeway for limes, and drops a bag of saltwater taffy on Carrie's lap when he returns. She chews on a piece, watching him.

Danya is talking shop. "So this guy wants to top himself because his girlfriend is threatening to enlighten his wife." She makes finger quotes around the word enlighten.

"So he's fucking around with the Buddha?" Carrie beams at her quick wit.

"The Buddha's a dude," Trev says.

"Not necessarily," Danya says. "More like an entity."

"Yeah Trev, ya sexist." Carrie shoves Trev. Leaves her hand. His skin is tingling. "What about all the statues in Nepal?"

Danya sighs. "He's not fucking the Buddha, he's fucking some bitch who gets nasty."

"So?"

"Thing is…" Danya pauses for effect. Her lipstick is smudged "He's realized he doesn't love either of 'em!"

"Drama!" Carrie pops another piece of saltwater taffy into her mouth.

"Still taste like shit?" Trev asks.

"Yeah." Her lips are stained blue.

Trev hands her a sliver of lime and a shot. "Wash it down with this."

Carrie takes the shot like a pro. Her cheeks are flushed. "Thanks." She stands, unsteady. "I think you should come with me. For a smoke," she adds quickly.

"Don't you want to hear the end of the story?" Trev isn't exactly sure what is happening.

"No." She presses hard against him.

"Okay." Now he's sure.

The bathroom is blue-tiled and Clorox bright. Carrie on her knees. It's over in minutes. Afterwards, Trev leans to kiss her, but she pulls away, eyes rolling back in the sockets. "No, no. I have a boyfriend."

They take different routes back to Danya's desk. Trev tells himself that this is a conquest. Whose conquest?

One drink.

"Last year, the phones started up at like, 12:01," Danya says. "It was weird."

"Like they were all waiting." Carrie nods. She's drinking water now, avoiding Trev's gaze.

Danya narrows her eyes at Carrie. Trev wonders if she can tell.

"We're ready for 'em!" Trev lifts his glass in a toast. He'll probably go a little further than he should, but that's all right. He's good at this. The Cuervo burns. It feels good. He can't remember the name of the song that is playing, but it's tight and percussive. Cocaine burns too, white hot on the way in, one fat line up each nostril. Burns down the back of your throat. Burns through your muscles, your arteries, your lymph. And before you know it, you've fallen in love with yourself. Finally.

Carrie and Danya are dancing. Rubbing against each other, and pulling away, as though suddenly bashful. Betty and Veronica. Trev pours a shot for Nat, and one for himself.

"Down the hatch," Nat says.

Trev swallows. "We haven't even been introduced. Trev." He wonders if she likes raw oysters with horseradish. Bungee jumping.

"Got any blow, Trev?" Her eyes are Alaskan black diamond.

"No." Trev pulls his cell out of his pocket. "I can make a call." He flips the phone in the air and catches it behind his back.

"I thought you might." She grins.

If you think you might harm yourself or someone else, hold the line.

"11:55!" Danya calls out.

Trev grabs Danya around her fleshy waist. Lets his hands sink into her. She shrieks and grabs Carrie in front of her, and a conga line begins. Nat's black fingernails digging into Trev's waist, finding their way beneath his belt.

Wind through the maze of cubicles. Digital displays and darkened server rooms and cables and paperwork.

"11:59!"

Circle the phones. Surrender and surrender and surrender.

"Whoever's closest to the phone has to answer it when it rings!"

"Yes!"

Midnight. They're ready.

Please hold the line. A counsellor is waiting for your call.

Imago

1. an insect in its final, adult, sexually mature, and typically winged state

2. an idealized mental image of another person or the self

A red wedding dress. Lightly patterned Chinese silk with a high neck and long train in the back. Jessica catches a glimpse of the dress when she pokes her head into Tina's room. Tina is rubbing her belly slowly, jutting it out and sucking it back in, frowning into a full-length mirror. Long, black hair loose and curled. There's a bouquet of long-stemmed white lilies on the dresser, tied with a ribbon.

"Ready when you are," Jessica says. When she doesn't receive an answer, Jessica smiles and closes the door. She wonders why Tina doesn't have any bridesmaids. As the groom's sister Jessica feels some responsibility to help with the ceremony but Tina hasn't asked for much. So, she's playing messenger.

Tina's family has a house in English Bay, so it's just a few steps across the street and down a path to the beach, where everyone is waiting. Tina's dad is on his way up, in an expensive suit rolled at the ankles.

"Finally ready?" he asks.

"She's all yours," Jessica says.

"Not for much longer." He looks just like Tina when he sulks, Jessica thinks. Sulk might not be the right word. Sulky. More like persistent malaise; Tina never smiles. Whatever. Jessica picks her way through the thin beach trail and joins the rest of the guests at the portable gazebo that Grant and his groomsmen spent an hour setting up last night. She gives the officiant—a heavyset woman with a big mole above her lip—the thumbs up.

There's no music, but Tina's sister has a Tibetan singing bowl that sends a weak monotone mewl across the sand as Tina and her dad approach. Of course, neither are smiling. They don't look angry or sad either, just...neutral. It's foggy—of course it's foggy Jessica thinks, it's the West Coast. Tina hasn't let the train on her dress out; she'd be dragging kelp and driftwood splinters—the tide came way up last night. Of course, there would have been time for the groomsmen to clear a path if the happy couple hadn't insisted on a sunrise wedding.

Tina has bare feet and Grant wears a suit with no tie. When they come together under the gazebo, it looks like they dressed in the dark. It's hard not to giggle at how awkward everything is—the officiant keeps losing her place and Tina's dad keeps sneezing. But when Tina and Grant exchange vows, even the brash seagulls shut up for a second. The crash of waves recedes into white noise. There's always that moment of togetherness, when the concept of *forever* seems doable. Jessica takes a Kleenex from her purse, hands one to her mother. After the kiss, there's a toast, and a seemingly endless demand for photographs. Jessica puts an arm around Grant's shoulders and he looks at her with tears

in his eyes. Little Grant, married. Then it's over, and the
flower girl makes a break for it, and throws Tina's bouquet
in the surf. Nobody seems to care.

Jessica has offered up her home for the reception. She
and her husband have a sixties-style place in the British
Properties, overlooking Vancouver. They ripped out the
kitchen when they moved in and renovated it in ultra-
modern white on white, but the rest of the house still has
that retro feel. Velvet wallpaper in the bathroom. Cement
pool out back, and a big patio. The kind of house Don
Draper would live in. Jessica doesn't think she's putting
herself out by offering to host the party, since she doesn't
see her brother as much of a social butterfly. In high school
Grant had been a glasses-wearing, Atari-playing nerd, who
collected beetles and pinned them into box frames. He sent
away to foreign countries for specimens. This was years
before online shopping. He mailed money orders to Brazil,
and they sent him dead bugs in little plastic eggs, to be
hatched like creepy aliens. Some of them had giant hook
beaks and others had iridescent shells, like gasoline spilled
into a puddle. He kept the star of his collection in a separate
frame—a big, crimson-coloured monster. Jessica wonders
what Tina thinks about the beetles. Did Grant hang them
above the bed? Gross.

Grant and Tina dated for five years. Around year three,
Tina planted some lavender bushes at Jessica's house, in the
planters next to the pool, and they grew like crazy. Long
porcupine spears of delicate, purple flowers that smell like
lemon soap. Jessica's gardener cuts them back, but they're
unstoppable. In the spring, they hum with honeybees. In
the late summer, Tina cuts and dries the flowers and makes
little underwear-drawer sachets for Jessica. Aside from

those sunny afternoons, Jessica sipping mint juleps by the pool while Tina cut lavender, they haven't really bonded. Jessica doesn't understand what interest Tina has in her brother. Grant always says they have a lot of fun together, but Jessica isn't sure what that means. Most young couples *think* they're a lot of fun. Jessica and her husband certainly did. Maybe they were. Now they just watch a lot of Netflix.

She waves to Tina and Grant as they get in the convertible Saab they've rented for the day. Grant waves back. "See you at mine," she mouths, but he's already looking elsewhere.

The reception setup begins right after the wedding. People carry in speakers, boxes of wine, decorations. Tina rushes around Jessica's living room in a pair of shorty-shorts and a tank top, her dress on a hanger in the bathroom. She moves three crates of Blue Mountain Brut into the library. Opens the French doors onto the patio. "This will be a good spot for the bar," she says. Six more crates follow: three red, three white.

"That's a lot of wine," Jessica says. Nobody answers. Three kegs are stacked against the wall next to the wine.

Grant is strutting around. "Put the turntables over there," he tells his groomsmen. Jessica knows one of them, Brian. When they were kids, Brian always followed Jessica around. Once, after swearing him to secrecy, she'd let him kiss her on the cheek. He and Grant had run a power washing business in ninth grade and invested the money they made in the stock market. Nerds.

"Turntables," she says to Brian.

"I've been spinning for years," he answers, batting his lashes. He's so lean and sharp-featured compared to the kid she remembers.

The chocolate fountain takes thirty minutes to get flowing. There are berries and melon and meringues. French macaroons and petit fours. Hazelnut florentines. Twinkies cut into little bite-sized pieces—Grant's request. A croquembouche cake—little cream puffs piled into a mountain and lacquered over with caramelized sugar. The sushi trays arrive. And then a popcorn machine. Jessica pours kernels and palm oil into the machine and turns it on. A cotton candy machine arrives. That is beyond her. It sits in a corner of the living room, unused.

"Grant," she says. "Isn't this a bit much?"

"No worries, Jess," he says.

"No worries!" Brian echoes, passing Jessica a flute of sparkling wine and clinking glasses with her. Jessica calls her husband and tells him to take the kids to his mother's. He should stay there too, she tells him, she'll make up some excuse. She doesn't want him to see this.

* * *

Tina slips into the bathroom at ten minutes to seven. She brushes a little bronzer on her cheeks and puts on her dress, runs a comb through her hair. That's all there's time for before the doorbell rings. She looks around for Grant, annoyed to be handling the receiving line alone. Most of the guests are his friends and family, he should be there to greet them. Her parents considered themselves done after the ceremony, no need to mingle with drunk strangers. Tina smiles and hugs people. She tells them where the bar is. Takes the gifts people have been told not to buy and stacks them on the table.

Between kisses and well-wishes, she inspects the food

table. Picks up an Earl Grey flavoured macaroon and takes a small bite. All this beautiful food and no appetite; she's been queasy all day. Her husband is on the far side of the pool, smoking a cigar-sized joint with a tight circle of friends. Even if she could smoke, it would make her shy and withdrawn. It doesn't have that effect on her husband. Nothing seems to.

When they first started dating, Grant took her to a lot of warehouse parties. Nobody called them raves, though that's basically what they were—a bunch of sweaty twentysomethings packed into an abandoned building. He seemed to know everyone, and everyone was strangely friendly, which Grant told her had a lot to do with the drugs. He told Tina he hadn't gone to his first party until college. She'd been a bit of a wallflower in high school too. Still is, she thinks, looking around at the chattering guests. Socializing has never been that important to her, but after she met Grant, she figured it should be. Still, she'd insisted that the wedding be family and close friends only. She didn't like the idea of being surrounded by spectators at such an intimate moment. Grant could do whatever he wanted at the reception, that was the deal.

After most people have arrived, Tina sets up the guest book. She special ordered the book from Italy. Polished oak covers and leather bindings, thick black pages. She bought white and silver pens from a stationery store on Granville Island. The Polaroid camera had been her grandmother's. The film had to be special ordered, since they don't mass-produce it any more. She looks around at the guests, and hopes she's ordered enough. Tina pulls a desk out onto the patio and covers it with a red tablecloth. She puts the book in the middle, and arranges some tea lights around it.

Cranberry scented. She puts the pens in a pewter mug and sprinkles some flower petals. Some of those sticky corners you use to secure photos in a book. The camera looks too modern, she thinks. She sprinkles some flower petals on it. A little printed sign mounted in a pewter frame says: *Sign the guest book and take a photo! Please limit yourself to two, so everyone gets a chance. Thanks! From the Happy Couple.*

Happy Couple shouldn't have been capitalized, she realizes. Oh well. She should really get mingling.

* * *

Jessica is roaming, collecting empty glasses and picking napkins up off the ground. Half-empty wine bottles crowd the tables, while guests continue to uncork more. She tells herself it's not her problem. More people are arriving; the front door has been propped open. She looks around for her brother, and finds him by deejay Brian, drinking Scotch out of one of the hand-blown glass espresso cups she brought back from Madrid last summer.

"I think you should wrap this up by one," she tells Grant.

He looks at her, bleary-eyed, flushed. "What's up, Jess?"

"I think it's for the best," she says.

He grips her arm and smiles, eyelids flutter a little. She doesn't see how he could possibly last past one anyway. Then Grant signals to Brian to stop the music, which he does with an exaggerated record scratch. People stop and look.

"Jess thinks we should wrap it up by one," Grant slurs, waving his arms over his head.

"The fuck?" somebody calls back. Jessica thinks the voice sounds familiar, maybe a cousin? Her hands clench but she keeps smiling, since all eyes are on them. After a pause, people start laughing, and they keep laughing until Brian puts the music back on.

"Jess, please." Her brother isn't smiling now. "At least until after Mack's set." Mack is Grant's other best friend, at least since college. He talks about Mack all the time.

"He's not here?" she asks.

"Mack needs to make an entrance," Grant says. "C'mon Jess." He tugs on her hand and hops back and forth like a kid.

"Two o'clock," Jessica says.

And then the patio doors swing open with such force they hit the walls with a crack. Three guys walk out towards the deejay table, holding square, aluminum suitcases. Two more guys follow. They seem to be clearing a path, not that it's necessary, since the crowd naturally parts to let a stocky guy come through. He has tattooed arms and a big metal piercing where his chin should be. Head shaved to avoid a bald spot. Two bored-looking girls follow.

Grant runs to the tattooed guy and hugs him, hugs the girls who suddenly become animated, shrieking and kissing him on the cheeks. Tina joins them, kisses and hugs like they haven't seen each other in years.

"We rented a limo!" the girls announce in tandem. The tattooed guy raises an arm in the air, fingers curled into devil horns. "The party starts now, bitches!" he says. The crowd shrieks in response.

Jessica pulls out her phone and dials her husband. She watches Mack's entourage elbow Brian out of the deejay spot. She wonders for a moment if there's going to be a fight, but Brian backs off willingly. A glass smashes behind her, and a woman laughs. *Oops!* somebody says. More laughter. Brian sees Jessica watching him, and gives her the thumbs up. She takes a breath, and hangs up the phone. This is not a big deal. She winds her way through the crowd and goes down to the basement, like her parents did when she used to throw parties in high school. Turns on the television. Upstairs, the music thumps.

A few minutes later, Tina pokes her head in. She's soaked, and still in her wedding dress. "Sorry," she says, "can I borrow some towels? We ended up in the pool." She follows Jessica to the laundry room.

"Is this going to end badly?" Jessica hands Tina an armload of beach towels. God, she sounds like her mother.

"No," Tina says. "I'm really sorry." She sheds her dress like snakeskin and wraps a towel around herself. "I'm pregnant."

"Oh, god," Jessica stammers, "congratulations! That's wonderful."

"Don't tell anyone," Tina says. "Not yet."

"No, of course not." It seems awkward to hug with Tina in a towel, but Jessica goes for it anyway. Yep, awkward. "Grant must be so... Grant knows, right?"

"About the baby? Of course."

"Of course, sorry. Of course. Hey, does Grant still have that beetle collection?" Jessica asks.

Tina blinks. "Beetle collection? Gross."

* * *

At two thirty, Tina decides that she and Grant have had enough. He's spread across a reclining deck chair, eyes rolled back in his head. A couple of Mack's girls keep reviving him. She tells them to go home. She finds more girls in the bathroom, snorting something off a mirror and taking photos of their boobs with the Polaroid. She tells them to go home.

"Can we keep the photos?" one of the girls asks.

"Sure," Tina says. God. This is why she doesn't have any girlfriends. Grant's friends are enough.

People are getting the hint—most have left. She pulls her new husband off the deck chair, takes off his wet clothes, and puts him to bed in the guest room Jessica made up for them. Sets the alarm clock. They've reserved a spot on the 9:00 a.m. ferry to Vancouver Island. "Don't worry," he slurs, "I'll be up in time."

"You're damn right you will be," she tells him. Kisses his snoring face. Puts on a sweater and goes back to the living room. Jessica's looking up from the bottom of the stairs. "Don't worry," Tina says. "I'll clean up."

"You do inside," Jessica says. "I'll do the patio."

Inside the house, Tina sorts the wine bottles into opened and unopened, and puts them back in the crates. Scrapes coagulated chocolate off plates, and stacks them in the rental trays. She remembers her wedding dress, in a wet lump on the floor. She runs downstairs to grab it, but Jessica's already hung it up in the shower. It's probably ruined, but what else would she have used it for anyway? The material is still fine for crafts, maybe. Those lavender sachets.

* * *

Outside, Jessica hangs wet tuxedo shirts on the clothesline, and dumps water out of black patent shoes. Empties ashtrays.

Brian is in the pool. "Are you the only one left?" Jessica says.

He looks up, frowning. "Some glass fell in the water."

Jessica finds the guest book, candle wax spilled down the

front, pages singed at the corners. *Happy Wedding, Bitches!* in silver ink, on the front page. A few pages in, other guests have posted their photos and well-wishes. Someone has drawn curly moustaches on them. Photos scattered around the table, including one of Mack and his entourage, naked from the waist down.

She exhales. Wraps the guest book in a plastic bag, separates the naked photos and throws them away. She'll go down to the artist's market at the quay in the morning and buy a photo album.

"Don't worry about the glass, really," Jessica says.

"No worries!" Brian winks at her. "Okay, maybe a few worries."

Jessica takes a pull on a half-empty bottle of wine and sits down on a chaise lounge across from Brian. "Did you know Tina was pregnant?" she asks, then regrets it.

Brian sort of choke-laughs. "Oh, uh, yes? No? I don't know how to answer."

"No, never mind, sorry." Jessica says.

"I mean, I noticed she wasn't drinking. I don't even know if she drinks—"

"Forget I said anything. And go home, really, I'll have the pool boy get it," Jessica says. But Brian keeps on his path, slow motion back and forth across the shallow end.

"She'll be good for Grant," he says. He's in his briefs, Jessica realizes, tighty-whities. She shouldn't feel weird, but she does. In the green pool glow, his chest and lean torso look like alien skin.

Radioactive Particles

I'm at St. Paul's hospital in Vancouver, with Maddie, reading *Archie* comics in the waiting room. Plastic chairs—Maddie's chubby legs don't reach the floor. She takes a pen and colours on the pictures so it looks like Veronica is missing teeth.

"Stop that," I hiss, even though there's no reason to keep my voice down. We're the only ones here. "Other people will want to read it."

"Shut up, ass-hat," Maddie says, without looking up. But she puts the pen in her pocket and leafs through the stack of *Choose Your Own Adventure* books Mom and Dad bought. I'm too old for them. My friends and I read *Cosmo*.

A nurse comes in and calls us both by name, even though we weren't introduced. She hands me a box of After Eight chocolates.

"You girls need a treat, and we have too many." She ruffles Maddie's hair. And then she turns on her heel, all business again.

"Thank you," I call after the nurse, but she doesn't hear me.

Maddie makes a swipe for the After Eights, but I hold them over her head. "You'll wreck your dinner." I assume we're having Christmas dinner. That's what people do on Christmas.

Maddie punches me in the thigh, to little avail. "Ass-hat."

The waiting room is crammed with dusty decorations: ornaments in teal and yellow, crumpled tinsel everybody reuses year after year even though it's only ninety-nine cents at the Dollarama. Over a fake fireplace, nine reindeer with kewpie doll eyes. Rudolph is covered in spray-on velvety red. We had the same ones when I was little, but Mom got rid of them. Christmas was a lot creepier in the seventies.

I peek into the hallway, wondering if the nurse knows whether the adults will be back soon. She's already gone. The lights are dimmed on the ward; Bing Crosby sings on the tinny radio about what a great time of the year it is. Teal garlands wind out of the waiting room like tentacles, down the hall towards Cousin Jens's room.

Cousin Jens is dying. Mom's cousin technically, not mine, but we don't bother with that, the family is too small. I don't have any cousins. And Jens is adopted, since aunt Helen couldn't have kids. In my baby photos, Jens is a young man—blonde and out of place among the olive-skinned Croatian side of the family. I'm in the centre with a Winnie-the-Pooh cake, then it's men on the left, women on the right. At family events, the women would stay in the kitchen, and the men would drink beer outside. That's how things went.

The adults are all clicking down the hall now: Mom and Dad and Aunty. Nobody really looks at Maddie or me. That's fine. I don't want to see them. I'm pretending like I'm not really here. I saw this film strip on Chernobyl at school, before Christmas break. A journalist that flew right over the meltdown said that when they passed through the stream of radioactive particles, he felt like he was leaving his body. Seeing everything from a long way away. I get that, feeling far away. In this whole stupid hospital, only the filaments in the Christmas lights are really in focus.

"I don't know what Alistair is doing here," Aunty says. "It should be family only."

Mom says something to Aunty, but I don't hear what. I wonder if Jens always felt outside of the family things too.

A nurse finally emerges from Jens's room and comes down the hall towards us. She beckons to the adults. There's a lot of nodding. Dad hugs Aunty, and then Mom. More nodding.

"Almost time," Dad says to us.

"For what?" Maddie asks.

"Shhh." He points for her to sit down, but she doesn't.

"For what?" she whispers as they file out of the room, heads bowed.

"Shhh," I say.

"You're an ass-hat." She kicks a fake present under the plastic tree. "A-s-s-h-a-t."

"Whatever." We're alone again.

We never really spent much time with Jens until he got sick. The first time we came to visit was about three months ago. In the car on the way to Vancouver, Mom asked Maddie and I if we knew what AIDS was. I told her a girl at school said I had AIDS when we were in a fight once. Dad let a few F-bombs go over that one. Mom said Aunt Helen might tell us that Jens had a tumour, but what he actually had was AIDS.

"Doesn't she know what's wrong with him?" Maddie asked, but Mom started to cry and nobody said anything.

I was pretty sure I knew what having AIDS meant, but I kept my mouth shut.

Hospital Jens looked a lot different from my baby pictures. Skinny. Old. He was mostly blind, but he smiled at us with straight white teeth from below a trimmed blonde moustache. He had gifts for us, posters from *Les Misérables*, signed by the cast.

"They all came to the hospital," he said. "It was fabulous!" Maddie snickered when he said fabulous. I poked her, hard in the ribs. Another man was there—Alistair—and he was holding Jens's hand. That's when I knew for sure Jens was gay. They're the only for sure gay people I've ever met. There might be one guy, in my class. But he denies it.

Jens took us to the Boathouse restaurant, where he worked before he got sick. Servers swarmed him with hugs and kisses and they gave us a table that looked out on English Bay. "How's the view?" he asked me. People walking dogs in bathing suits and short-shorts. I tried to make it sound like he wasn't missing much.

I looked through the menu and realized I didn't know what anything was. Jens told me to read out the name of each dish, and he explained.

"Carpaccio di Manzo?"

"Shaved raw beef in vinaigrette. To die for."

"Ewwww," Maddie said.

"I'll have that," I said, hoping I sounded fabulous. But Mom ordered us the mulligatawny soup instead. Jens lit the wrong end of a cigarette and it flared up. Dad had to grab it and throw it in a glass of water. Mom helped him light the second one. Maddie, who always made a fuss when Mom smoked in a restaurant, kicked my leg under the table.

"Take me to the bathroom," she said.

I kicked her back.

There were hand lotions and hairspray and orchids, things we'd never seen in a public washroom.

"Cousin Jens is kind of weird," Maddie said.

"I think maybe because he's gay," I said. "Or maybe it's the AIDS."

After dinner, Mom took me aside.

"If you ever realize that you're gay, you can tell us, and we'll love you and accept you," she said.

"What about Maddie?" I asked.

"She's too young," Mom said.

Not long after that, Jens went into a coma.

I'm hungry. I sit on the floor and peel the cellophane away from the box of chocolates.

"You'll wreck your dinner," says Maddie, doing her best mom voice.

"Who cares?"

She squeals and squats down. We're conspirators, allies in the league of wrecked dinners. Now it's *A Charlie Brown Christmas* on the radio. The chocolates go down, one after another, with barely time to savour. By the time Dad comes to get us, we've eaten them all.

"Time to say goodbye," he says. He takes Maddie's hand.

Follow the teal tentacles to Jens's room. There's no one at the nurses' station, nobody in the halls. It's past ten, the hall clock says, so dinner is already ruined. Good thing we ate the chocolates.

There's a sink right outside the room, since you're not supposed to bring any germs in. I lean down to turn the tap on, but Dad waves me away.

"No need, sweetie," he says.

I guess Jens really is going to die.

The air in the room is thick, like it's full of radioactive particles. And I do feel far away, even though I should feel right here. There's a hissing in my ears, like when a record is over. Jens is propped up on the pillows Aunty embroidered, eyes closed. I should hold his hand the way Mom does, the way Alistair did. All the adults are lined up on either side of him so I can't get close enough. A bunch of fuzzy, sad faces looking at me and Maddie like I should do something.

"Goodbye cousin—" Maddie starts, in a loud voice, but I pinch her shoulder. She looks up at me, confused, and I wish we were back in the waiting room again. Then Jens makes a sound and his body starts to shake and everything is motion. Dad's yelling; Aunty, Maddie, and I are hustled back out to the hall, and the door closed behind us.

"Be kind, rewind," Maddie says. She's walking backwards, retracing her steps down the hall. Her hand grasps at my hip. "Did you say goodbye in your head?" she asks.

"I didn't have time."

"How are you going to say it?" Maddie asks.

"Tell him we love him and accept him." When I say it out loud it sounds kind of cheesy.

Our spots on the waiting-room floor are still warm. We sweep the chocolate wrappers into the wastebasket. I let Maddie unwrap a fake present, even though we both know there's nothing inside. At the waiting-room windows, she and I scratch our names in the spray-on snow, and peek through to the parking lot. There's real snow falling outside, thick sugary flakes that I hope will last until after we say goodbye.

Honeybee Dance

Cass needs to have the right moment with Harry before he dies. She's not sure what it will be. Most weekends, they sit on the back porch at his place. After Cass's mother died, Harry bought two properties in the country. Harry's house is a split-level rancher. Cass's place is a willowy farmhouse, like something out of a prairie romance. Only a short bike ride between them. Cass rode over this morning, with a basket of muffins and some thimbleberry jam. Harry made tea.

"Remember when I showed you that fruit fly crawling across the table, and you squished it?" Cass asks him. "And I started to cry."

"No." Harry frowns.

"I want you to know that I know I overreacted," Cass says.

"That's okay." He pats her hand.

Now Cass frowns. Forgiveness is not what she's looking for, though she does feel guilty. She was seven years old, watching the fruit fly make its way across the yellow Formica. Feeling proud of herself for not responding with the typical disgust that most girls her age had for bugs. She was observing. Like a scientist. The fruit fly seemed spent, wings fluttering but never taking off, winding a drunkard's path around the marmalade. She wondered if marmalade was as nourishing as fresh fruit for a fruit fly. She thought about what the world must look like from tiny bug eyes. And when she pointed out the fruit fly to her dad, she wanted him to wonder about those things with her. Thinking he'd been summoned as pest control, Harry crushed the fruit fly with his thumb. Tears came faster than Cass could suppress, snotty mewls that brought her mother running from the living room. From her mother's lap Cass watched Harry shake his head, hands held up in surrender as he left the room. At the time, Cass thought Harry deserved it; women on one side, him on the other.

The geraniums Harry buys by the flat at Walmart every spring reach for the morning sun from their plastic cups. Beg to be moved to the planters out front. A fat marmot pokes its head out of the wood pile and sniffs. The neighbour's dog barks, spooks it back under.

"They whistle to each other through their front teeth when there's danger," Harry says. He tells her this every time they see the marmot. Harry was an English teacher before he retired, but he loves nature shows.

"Remember that time you whistled for a waitress at that restaurant, and she tried to give you attitude about it?" Cass says.

"I whistled at her?" Harry puts down his teacup. He stopped drinking coffee after his last visit to the doc. Claimed he preferred orange pekoe anyway.

"We'd been waiting there forever, and nobody served us," Cass says.

He laughs. "That doesn't sound like me."

Cass takes a muffin from the basket. Chews and swallows. The book she read when her mother got sick—*Synergistic*

Grieving—called the connection you're supposed to have with someone before they die *synergistic understanding*. When two people speak and listen and really see each other. Cass read that book in the eighties, when everything from mental health to soft drink refreshment was measured in synergy. Readers loved the book, and so did critics. It was the first thing she thought of when Harry got the diagnosis a few months ago. The author of *Grieving Before Death* has a new book that revisits the grief process, but now synergistic understanding is called mindful connection. Keeping up with the current lingo is important, since people won't listen to outdated-sounding advice. Otherwise, it's pretty much the same; the book outlines five easy steps to mindful connection. Clearing up past misunderstandings is step two. So far Harry has confounded all of the steps.

It's okay, Cass thinks. Harry's still got months ahead of him yet, maybe years, not like when her mother got sick and was gone in three days. This is just a rehearsal.

When she's not visiting Harry, Cass tends to her bees. She keeps three hives at the back of her property. Every spring she uses a pneumatic nail gun to assemble the kits she buys from an apiarist supply in the States. Ka-shunk. Ka-shunk. Ka-shunk. Ten nails for one hive, each carefully lined up so the wood doesn't split. She paints each box yellow and blue.

When the paint is dry, Cass slips nine frames in each hive box, like hanging files. Each frame holds a thin sheet of beeswax, stamped with a hexagon pattern. A blueprint. If the bees follow the blueprint, each frame fills up evenly with hexagon cells. The bees fill the cells with honey, and cap them with wax. Most of the time they fill the entire frame with precision. But sometimes they go rogue, and the frame is chunky on one side and empty on the other. Cells running over onto the walls of the hive, so Cass has to cut them out with a warm knife. This is when she checks in with the bees. Asks them how everything is going. Any problems with the queen? Any stressors: a cold spring or damp summer? She meditates a little first. Puts her bare hands on the hive and breathes deep. Sometimes the bees crawl on her fingers. She's been stung a few times. When she was a kid, a sting always felt personal. How could something so grand and benevolent as nature attack her? That part hurt more than the stingers ever did.

Cass keeps bees because she's worried that they're disappearing. She's worried about colony collapse disorder—when the workers leave their hives and don't come home. People say it's the radiation from cell phone towers, or it could be pesticides. Maybe it's the beekeepers who transport hives all over the country on flatbeds to rent out to farmers. Bees hate change. But none of these theories can explain why they disappear completely, no telltale pile of dead workers at the hive site. Beekeepers find the queen all but abandoned.

Cass read somewhere that Einstein said if the bees disappear, the world won't last five years. So she keeps her own bees, and tries to keep them happy. Gives the excess honey away at Christmas, or trades her neighbour for farm fresh eggs.

Harry's geraniums are for Cass's bees. It's the only reason the cedar planters get filled every year. Otherwise, the garden has gone to pot: leggy daffodils push up like clockwork in the spring and fall over, morning glory chokes the roses. Cass helps Harry pull the geraniums one by one out of the flats and collect the plastic garden markers into a pile. He memorized the cultivation instructions a long time ago: full sun, water every two days. A couple of rocks at the bottom of each planter for drainage, then soil. They work at dusk, so the transplanted flowers have time to recoup before the sun hits them. Cass uses her mother's old watering can. Harry takes a drink from the hose each time he bends to fill it up for her. They look so much alike: ruddy skin, deep-set eyes, nostrils big enough to fit a marble in.

When they're done outside, Harry puts the kettle on.

Cass pulls the fancy teacups her mother never used out of the cupboard. "If you have regrets, you should let them go," she says. Step four, letting go.

"What kind of regrets?" He burps. Cass has him taking Omega-3 oil and it gives him gas.

"I have regrets," Cass says. "Quitting piano lessons. Cheating on boyfriends."

Harry pauses over the fancy cups but pours the tea anyway. "That's fine."

"Did you ever cheat on a girlfriend?" she asks.

The sugar spoon clatters. "Of course I never cheated. On anyone."

She's provoked him, but the opening spurs Cass on. "Do you regret not really getting to know your dad?" When Harry's father got cancer, he converted and refused to speak to anyone who wasn't born-again Christian. Even on his deathbed.

"I can thank my dad for the cancer," Harry says. "That's enough."

"Do you think that's true? It's inherited?"

He grunts. "Daughter of mine, be thankful you don't have a prostate."

Hearing the words *cancer* and *prostate* in such close proximity makes Cass swallow. They sit back outside. Watch the marmot shamble across the yard to the lilac bush.

"They whistle—"

"—I know, Dad."

"How are the bees?" Harry asks.

She puts a hand on her chest. "Stressed lately."

"Remember your training." He pats her knee.

There is such a thing as a bad hive. Aggressive guards who buzz the ears of anyone nearby. Hover at eye level, like they're trying to stare you down. Stinging is always a last resort, since the bees lose their life. But there are colonies that send out kamikaze fighters at the slightest provocation. Cass has seen a bad hive, when she worked at a farm in Chilliwack— before she had her own colony.

As she opened the hive box for a routine check, they poured out and covered her bee suit and bonnet. She almost dropped the lid and ran but, worried that would make things worse, she hung on, completely blinded by the onslaught of tiny bodies surrounding her. Their presence alone was frightening, but there was something about the particular sound they made, angrier and more aggressive than anything she'd ever experienced. Bee suits are cumbersome and hot—sweat collected around the rim of her bonnet and rolled down her temples. Adrenaline pumped. In desperation, she mentally assembled a list of steps for *Complex and/or Aggressive Bee Communication*. Don't swing your arms around. Don't look at the bees crawling on the netting inches from your face. Get inside your body, see your fear as a light and snuff it out. Controlled breath. Acceptance of the moment. All those hackneyed self-help mantras are there for a reason. As she walked away from the hive, the bees retreated, unwilling to be too far from the queen. So in a way, she walked it off. Harry gets a kick out of this, the walking it off part. He calls this her "training."

"I remember," Cass says. Harry nods.

Cass pushes the pedals on her bike; she's on her way home. She remembers to feel the contraction of the muscles in her legs and the tightness in her lungs. She hears the transport trucks on the highway and the *chick chick chick* of irrigation sprinklers in the alfalfa fields. The pockets of cool, heavy air they create in the evening warmth. She stops thinking about what the right moment looks like.

The alfalfa rolls like sea grass in the wind, but it's still now. Her bees love it, and there's no shortage in the valley. But she's sure that when they reach Harry's geraniums every spring, that's when the party starts. The first scouts touch down on the pink blooms and taste. Such exotic nectar, after a long winter of sugar water. They fill their saddlebags with pollen and fly home to tell the others. They pass Cass on her bike, forever in transit between her own house and Harry's. Coast up and down the driveway in her slipstream.

When the bees who've tasted Harry's geraniums get to the hive, they're met at the door by guards watching for foreigners like wasps, or even bees who come from other hives to rob honey. The guards smell the new nectar, brush some pollen from the worker's antennae. Soon the hive hums with a vibration that calls the colony home.

And Cass's bees will always come home, she thinks, pulling the bike into the garden shed. Stepping out and closing the padlock. They'll come home from the neighbours' fancy imported magnolias, wrapped in burlap every winter so they don't freeze. From the alfalfa fields, blowing and rolling like sea grass. They come home for the sake of the hive and—she believes this though she's never seen it in any beekeeping book—they come home for the dance. This is what bees do when there's something important to say.

Inside the hive, nurse bees and drones gather around. Even the queen makes an appearance. There are other dancers, those who have discovered foxglove at city hall, or sunflowers near the park. Attentive workers stay close, butting up against the dancers, judging for themselves who makes the best case. Harry's geranium advocates waggle their bodies at a precise angle between his house and the sun. It's inefficient, might take hours to let the number of turns tell the story. Turn to the left. Waggle. Turn to the right.

Moosehide

It's the middle of the day, who cares when exactly, grey on goddamn grey. According to the GPS, we just passed the Arctic Circle. People get out their iPhones to take pictures of each other—Sean takes mine since we're paddling together—and when I smile for the camera I feel a little bit happy. Or I tell myself I feel happy. Technically, this is an accomplishment, paddling a million kilometres in the cold, past an arbitrary line on a map that raises eyebrows when you mention it to your fellow urbanites.

Sean and I both have to reach as far as we can across the canoe when he passes me the phone, to give my approval of the photo. The skin on his hands is cracked and scratchy; not the accountant's hands he had two weeks ago. The gaunt face glowing back at me from the iPhone looks pretty happy. I've lost weight. I guess that will make me happy when I get back to Vancouver and put on my skinny jeans. When I only have to wear one layer at a time, and people can see how skinny I've really become. For now, in all these layers, I'm a skinny face popping out of the Michelin Man. I take Sean's picture with the phone. He looks handsome. Of course, there's no WiFi, so I just save the photos. If you're in the Arctic, and you can't Instagram it, does anybody care?

I'm tired.

Early in the trip, the river was all crusty whitewater. I was always paddling a canoe into a bunch of waves that looked like they were beating the shit out of each other. The water roared, and I could hear it all the time. I was excited by the noise at first, but I got used to it. At night, it was a backing track for Sean's evening banjo serenades. The guides had glanced sideways at each other when he'd added the bulky case to the packing pile, but everyone is happy to listen to him pluck away most evenings.

It's all couples on the trip: three couples and the guides, Jan and Eric. Also a couple. At night, besides the sound of the river, I can hear people rolling around in their tents, groaning like whales. Sean and I tried to get busy the first night, but my back muscles felt like they'd been run through a food processor. Same thing the second night, and the Thermarest deflated, so I was being pounded onto the rocks. Ugh. Around day six, I pulled Sean into the trees, away from everyone and down into a valley dotted with little white flowers. There was this spot with moss so thick, we had to climb up onto it. The whole thing was so badass; we weren't supposed to stray out of sight of the group, and we weren't supposed to go anywhere that might mess up the nature. The tundra is fragile, that's what the guides told us. We were stomping around, ripping out chunks of moss, and when I pulled him down to me, the sanctity of nature was the last thing from my mind. But the cold rose up from the ground, deep and penetrating. Sean put his jacket underneath me. We kept as many layers on as we could, his hard dick poking out of wool long johns, my own base layer pulled just low enough to let him in. But we couldn't stop shivering. A handjob under the majestic northern sky just seemed sad, and besides, we'd forgotten to bring wet wipes.

"We'll get it," Sean said. Kissed me on the forehead.

"Yeah."

The other couples are from Toronto, a zillion times more urban than us. I don't know why they don't seem to have any trouble getting it. From the sound of it, they're getting it constantly.

The river has slowed since we left Aberdeen Canyon, it's big and sluggish and muddy now. For the most part, the only sound comes from the nattering of our fellow travellers, and this only happens when we're rafting, boats tied together. Sometimes the wings of birds make a *whoop whoop whoop* sound when we startle them into flight. The couples don't mingle much anymore, and I'm not sure if that's because we're comfortable with each other now, or because we've given up.

When we pull off the river, the moosehide is just laying there. God. Big, inflated lungs laying next to it, jiggling like jello. Intestines, veiny grey tubes.

"Why is everything inflated?" I ask Sean.

"Botulism," somebody says.

"Don't poke a hole in them," somebody says, "or the worst smell will come out."

How bad, I wonder?

The worst.

Brown-winged birds of prey circle over us.

Everybody loves the hide, prodding and poking it with sticks. Stretching it out so they can see the full length of the inside, mucus membrane and pink blood, a skin cape cut ragged around the edges. I can't look at it. I don't see a dead moose, I see a live moose in the final moments of suffering before its life ends. That kind of empathy is stupid. I know. The moose is dead, and it's feeding someone.

Somebody's going to notice that I'm the only one not looking, and ask me why I'm such a wuss. So I make a big show of looking at other things: tiny plants at the river's edge with ice globes surrounding the fruit, broken willow branches, rocks. Scarred rocks that look like patients in the sick ward; what makes them look like that? I toss a few in the river. Each lands with a fat *plunk*.

Sean's talking to Eric about taking the moosehide with us and I'm pissed at him for this. Surely bears would smell it and come looking for us, or lynx, or—what else is out here waiting to kill us? He wants to make something out of it. Whatever. I remember somebody in my Aboriginal Studies class saying that scraping a hide is much harder than it looks, even with expert hands, and we're no experts. We have no tools for this. I may be a mixed blood—Sean and I are both Cree-Métis—but we were also both raised white. All we know are white-people things. But I do know that a perfectly good moosehide shouldn't have been left here. Why did the hunters leave it? Skin it and leave it?

"I think it's a female," somebody says, poking around the ass end, playing the expert.

"You're not supposed to kill females," somebody says.

"That's sexist," somebody says.

"The females make more moose, dumbass."

"Not without sperm they don't."

"Maybe she attacked them?"

God. It's like reading the online comments section on YouTube.

I'm hungry.

Somebody passes around a snack, just a big block of

cheese cut into a million pieces with a dirty Leatherman. It clogs and sticks in my throat. We get "fun-sized" Mars bars too. Chocolate and cheese. I put the Mars bar in my PFD pocket. My fingers can barely get the zipper down. My fingers, dirty for days despite a river of hand sanitizer. Bloated and pus around the nails, one finger swollen so big I can barely move it. Rub Polysporin in the cracks before bedtime, and hope for the best. I can still paddle just fine. I may have lost weight, but my shoulders are strong now. I can feel the muscle through my merino wool bottom layer, though I haven't seen much of my actual skin for fifteen days.

"Can you help me with my PFD?" Sean asks. He looks like a little boy when he asks, and for some reason I choke up a little. Get it together, lady.

"Sure," I say. Tug the zipper down hard, even though my fingers might break off.

"Do you want my Mars bar?" he asks.

"Don't drag that moosehide along with us," I say.

"I could make a drum from it."

I turn around so he doesn't see how hard I'm rolling my eyes. A drum. We're *accountants*.

Now it's pictures around the moose remnants, eight of us lined up like so many soldiers. Someone's found an antler, too. Not from the carcass, this one's older. And probably caribou, Eric tells us. People take turns with it, more photo opportunities.

Sean's arm around me, the other holding the antler up to my temple. We'll get back to Vancouver and show this photo to our friends, and they'll be jealous of us. I can't even count how many times people used the word jealous, like we were going on an expenses-paid five-star Mediterranean yacht cruise or something. You'd have to be a masochist to want to trade places with us right now. There is nothing easy about being here, and there was nothing easy about getting here. Sean and I trained for months, saved for months. I guess it was good for us to have something to focus on. We barely fought at all. I'm not sure if we picked the right kind of vacay. I'm not sure if it's just the tour we chose, because I've never done anything like this before. But I definitely didn't expect things to be this hard. I pictured myself drinking wine, looking out at the river. I'd imagined calm, and a clearing out of my mind that might make the future easier to see. Anyway. We're doing it now. We're committed.

Time to get back in the boats. It's much warmer when I'm paddling, tied into the spray skirt with my neoprene gloves on. Sean and I always paddle together now. Early in the trip when there was some pretense of friendship among travellers, people switched up paddle mates and made small talk, but not any more. I don't really care. My friends back home told me this kind of trip forges lifelong connections, so maybe there's something wrong with me.

People take their last pokes at the moose bits. Somebody finally does poke a hole in the lung and it deflates unceremoniously, no smell. One of the guides finally convinces Sean that bringing the pelt along is a stupid idea, but I'm still annoyed so I'm not speaking to him. He points out the same shit we've seen for the last week: stunted trees, exfoliated hills, mud. I just paddle.

When it's finally time to find camp for the night, the atmosphere is thick. The river so still it looks like mercury.

"Taco Bar tomorrow," Eric says.

"Is that some kind of sick joke?" Sean asks. He gets grumpy when I give him the silent treatment.

Eric laughs. "Taco Bar is a checkpoint," he says. "If you need anything flown in or flown out, that's the spot."

"How 'bout some tacos," somebody says. "Hur hur hur."

"They'd be some pretty expensive tacos," Eric says. "Airlift costs about three grand."

"That's our way out," I say to Sean. So much for the silent treatment.

He snorts. "Kiss that ring goodbye then."

I shrug, knowing it's going to piss him off. He looks at me and laughs. People say travelling together is a true test of a relationship. Those people are correct.

"SMOKE," a voice bellows from a canoe behind me. "SMOKE."

I realize I've been looking right at the smoke for a few minutes, but it hasn't registered. "Smoke," I say to Sean.

"No shit."

"Smoking Hill," Eric says. "Lightning hit a coal seam in the mountain, it's been burning ever since." This generates a lot of delighted conversation. In the absence of internet, I guess we're all pretty easily amused. "Let's stop here tonight," Eric says.

We begin the transition back to land-dwelling mammals: pull the boats up, loosen the spray skirt laces, pull out the gear. Although everyone is tired, this is when we work together best, since the end goal of sleep is finally in sight. The mud is too thick to slog through with a heavy pack, so a line forms, and we pass everything along. Bag after bag: tents, cooking gear, food. Empty boats carried safely above the water line. Sean and I set up the camp kitchen. I find rocks for a hearth while he collects firewood. Then he builds the fire while I sort through the food barrels for tonight's meal. When everyone else is done with their tasks, they'll all come and circle us like vultures.

"We could leave," Sean says.

"What?"

"We could." He blows into the fire and sparks fly out. "We could split the three grand and get the fuck out of here."

The water is boiling. I measure out three cups of par-boiled rice and dump it in. "Why?"

Sean snorts. "It was your idea."

"We might be waiting a while, I doubt there's a shuttle," I say, watching the rice come to a boil. Fire cooking is not what you'd call precise, but I'm getting better at it.

"I asked Eric," Sean says. "He could call on the satellite phone."

"We could." I think about what our friends would say. It would look like a failure. But they have no idea how hard every day has been. They probably wouldn't *say* much at all, but they would think I'd failed.

"I mean, this is our *vacation*," Sean says. "It's not supposed to be work."

"We could hit that spa in Whitehorse and get four-handed massages."

Sean laughs. "How about six-handed."

"I like the way you think," I say. We kiss for the first time in a million years.

"Wooo, get a room you two," somebody calls. The vultures are descending.

"A room," Sean says. "We could get one. Think about it."

I do think about it. What heat would feel like. Electric light. Hot water on demand. Mealtime rolls into fire time, people roast marshmallows and laugh among themselves.

In the distance, Smoking Hill is glowing a little, and still sending up a thin, white plume into the night sky. It's a long time before the sky gets dark, and usually by then the northern lights are out. Green streaks across a deep blue twilight. They were so exciting at first, now we just expect them. But tonight, the idea that this could technically be my last night out here has got me looking around again, noticing things.

"Meet you in the tent," Sean says, kissing my cheek.

"I'll be there in a bit," I say.

"Don't be too long, we've got stuff to discuss." He lopes off toward our coffin-sized tent. Handsome.

I leave my comrades at the campfire, but instead of going straight to the tent, I end up down at the edge of the river, looking at the burning hill. Big moon. Me in the mud. It's so shitty out here. But still, technically, this is romance. It's hard to remember that, since we're always moving on this stupid river, or too exhausted to think. I stand still for awhile. Try to imagine getting picked up by an airplane tomorrow. Removing all future responsibility from ourselves in one simple but expensive manoeuver. Crawling into the plane and laughing together like Benjamin and Elaine on the bus at the end of *The Graduate*. Escape! Ha ha ha. Ha ha.

Ha.

Well.

What now?

Acknowledgments

This book was written on the traditional, ancestral, unceded territories of the Musqueam, Squamish, and Tsleil-Waututh peoples, on which I am a grateful guest.

To my fam, you guys rule. Brian and Karen and everyone at Anvil. UBC creative writing. Wayde and Betsy and everyone at The Writer's Studio at SFU. Calvin and Liz and the Douglas College creative writing program, and *EVENT* Magazine. Ben, Laura, Tasha and Sarah for listening to my stories and my neuroses in equal parts and loving me anyway. To the stitch & bitch gals: Jess, Anne and Gillian, for the same. My Book Warehouse peeps: Mary-Ann, Talia and James—team us guys. My Odin Books peeps, who emphatically insist I have something to offer.

Jónína Kirton, Jon Paul Fiorentino, Chris Evans, Tim Taylor. Thank you.

Janet, Patrik, Jocelyn, Mica, Tyler, Ben, Leena, Kiri, Kyle, Mallory, Claire and Rob, and some folks already mentioned, for helping me out in a pinch. Some of you, more than once.

And to Katie Green Watercolour Machine, for the incredible cover art.

Thank you to everyone who has supported me, and to everyone who supports small presses.

I would also like to thank the editors of the following magazines and journals where some of the stories first appeared:

"War of Attrition" and "The Modern Intimate" in *Joyland*; "Shoe Shopping with the Cash Poor," "Last Call," and "Chins and Elbows" in *subTerrain*; "Read These Postcards in a Gonzo Journalist Voice" in *Matrix*; "Moosehide" in *THIS Magazine*.

ABOUT THE AUTHOR

Carleigh Baker is a Cree-Métis/Icelandic writer. She was born and raised on the traditional, ancestral, unceded territory of the Stó:lō people. She won the Lush Triumphant award for short fiction in 2012, and her work has also appeared in *Best Canadian Essays*, and *The Journey Prize Anthology*. She writes book reviews for the *Globe & Mail*, *The Literary Review of Canada*, and *The Malahat Review*. She currently lives as a guest on the traditional, ancestral, unceded territory of the Musqueam, Squamish, and Tsleil-Waututh peoples.